I0741500

THE GIVING OF US

THE GIVING OF US

When Broken Strangers Find Healing
Through Horses and Each Other

Glenna Shawn

COPYRIGHT © 2025 GLENNA SHAWN
All rights reserved.

THE GIVING OF US
When Broken Strangers Find Healing Through Horses and Each Other

FIRST EDITION

ISBN 978-1-5445-4992-7 *Hardcover*
978-1-5445-4991-0 *Paperback*
978-1-5445-4993-4 *Ebook*

Contents

Chapter One

THE EARLY DRIVERS ON ROUTE 29 WERE ENJOYING THE morning light. The air was crisp, and the sun was warm.

Driving at top speed, Tim felt his first thrill of the day. It was a better adrenaline rush than his morning coffee. As he drove, he relished the air, the scenery, and especially the feeling of the sweet-smelling wind blowing through his hair and the sun on his face. His morning commute to the city was his favorite part of the day—most mornings he didn't even turn on his radio. It was such a pleasure to listen to the birds, the wind, and the intoxicating sound coming from the twelve-cylinder engine of his sports car.

He was the first to hear the grinding of metal against metal and then metal against pavement. As he rounded the slight bend in the road, Tim saw an eighteen-wheeler on its side sliding toward him. Smoke and sparks shot from the truck as the metal scraped along the highway. Flames flew out from the back.

Tim reacted immediately, slamming on the brakes and

steering toward the road's right shoulder. His many weekends training with instructors at the racetrack in West Virginia allowed him to stay calm despite the truck flying toward him— at least as calm as could be expected. Tim analyzed his situation and put all his attention on controlling the vehicle. Cargo flew in all directions over the highway as the truck careened down the road. As Tim watched with bated breath, the semi moved closer to his car.

The truck began to slow, but not quickly enough to avoid a collision. There was no way to maneuver around the oncoming vehicle. Tim immediately put the car in reverse. He threw his right arm over the passenger seat, looked to the rear, and slammed his foot on the gas. He was careful not to oversteer and cause his car to flip. He didn't dare to turn his head and check how far the truck had come; he needed his full attention on his driving. Tim listened as the truck scraped along the highway, tearing up guardrails and grinding over pavement. He desperately hoped to hear silence soon.

The truck finally ground to a halt, and Tim stopped his car. He breathed a ragged sigh of relief. At the same time, several other cars reached the same spot on the highway and joined him at a full stop. All faced the behemoth that was lying on its side, blocking every lane. The drivers remained in their cars for several moments, staring at the horrific scene in front of them.

The damaged central island looked as if a bulldozer had driven through the area. The truck had crashed through at top speed.

Soon, several people jumped out of their cars to see if anyone was injured. Some were already on their phones dialing 911. One of the drivers, Jeff, leaped from his car and ran back toward the bend in the road to alert oncoming traffic so that others would have time to stop. Another, Michele, while frightened to get too close, hurried toward the large truck to see if she could help the driver. She was relieved when he crawled out the window, seemingly uninjured.

In thirty minutes, the highway was full of trucks, flashing lights, and first responders wearing bright-yellow vests. As many as twenty people swarmed the truck and the debris spread across the highway. The lead responder leaned his head toward his shoulder to speak into his radio.

"All personnel, don your masks now. There are fumes rising off the roadway. Those with cars on the highway, turn them around and get them out of the area. We have a hazmat situation. Do it now!"

Chapter Two

TIM HAD GOTTEN AN EARLY START ON WHAT PROMISED to be a very busy day. He loved the frantic pace at work and the serenity that surrounded him when he was home. A career in finance kept him immersed in an exciting world of client meetings and business lunches. Tim usually arrived at his office before any of the other people in his firm and went straight to work reading the financial reports that had come in overnight. By the time a few employees arrived in the office, he was up to speed on just about everything. At nine o'clock it was time to start working the phones.

Today, all he could do was turn around and go home. His wife, Sharon, would be there, as she worked remotely as a cartoonist.

Driving away from the wreckage, he longed to go home, a place of peace and quiet.

Chapter Three

AS MICHELE TURNED HER CAR AROUND, SHE PICTURED
her home to help calm her nerves. She could not imagine living
anywhere else but on Mountain View Road, in the farmhouse
where she grew up. The home had been in her family for generations. After pulling into her driveway, she sat in her car for a
few moments to look at her place. The sun was shining, lighting
up the flowers lining the front walk. The house exuded such a
feeling of warmth and security.

Michele lived there with her only son, Sam, the product of
a forgotten night with an old beau seven years ago. She loved
Sam with all her being and hoped that the farm would be a
home for him and his family for years to come. Her job in the
city provided the money needed for necessities, and she didn't
mind the time it took to drive in each day to make her idyllic
life on the farm possible. Every morning after the school bus
picked Sam up, Michele headed to work for a publisher of
several specialty magazines.

Chapter Four

JEFF RETURNED TO HIS HOME ON MOUNTAIN VIEW ROAD after witnessing the accident. He was in his final months as an employee, looking forward to his retirement just around the corner. He and his wife, Dell, had waited many years to be able to spend day upon day sitting on their front porch and admiring the mountain view.

Jeff was a quiet and kind man. Because he grew up on a farm and spent many hours by himself or with the horses his family raised, he knew the importance of paying attention to his surroundings without being center stage himself.

The drive home took about twenty minutes, so Jeff tuned in to his favorite country station, lowered his windows to feel the breeze, and enjoyed the beautiful morning sun.

Jeff sold farm machinery for a living. The job allowed him to provide for a family and afford his home in the country. It could be a difficult job because he knew that most farmers were not wealthy, and the machines were very expensive. It took a great deal of sensitivity to help find financing without offending his clients. Sometimes he contacted neighboring farmers to see if several wanted to pool their resources to purchase the necessary equipment. Jeff's job was not all the way in the city, but he wouldn't mind when he no longer needed to commute every day.

Chapter Five

AS TIM PULLED INTO HIS DRIVEWAY, HE SAW A CAR HE didn't recognize. Perhaps his wife had invited a friend for lunch. He hoped she wouldn't mind setting another place at the table and, more importantly, that she had enough food for one more person. Lunch outside on such a beautiful day was a bonus. After such a harrowing experience, now that Tim was home, he started to relax. It was like a snow day, only better.

Tim entered the house and was puzzled by the quiet. Perhaps Sharon and her guest or guests were outside. Where was all the chatter that usually accompanied a get-together with friends? He roamed through the first floor and saw no one. Maybe Sharon and her friend had gone out and Sharon had driven.

Tim decided it was best for him to change from his office clothes and maybe take care of some minor chores he had been putting off for a long time.

As Tim reached his bedroom, he was surprised to see the door closed. It was almost never closed, even when they slept at night.

Whatever, he thought. *Quit stalling and change your clothes.* He reached for the door and pushed it open.

When he entered his bedroom, he saw his beautiful wife sleeping, and as he walked over to give her a kiss, his eyes adjusted to the low light.

She was in the arms of another man.

The shock forced him to his knees and knocked all the air from his lungs. Covering his mouth to quiet his gasp, he pushed himself up off the floor. Tim backed out of the room, quietly closed the door, and stood still, listening to the pounding of his heart. All he wanted was to believe he had not seen what he had just seen, but he knew there was no mistake.

In the hallway, he could only think, *What do I do? What do I do? What do I do?* The ache in his chest was so strong he felt there was a clamp wrapped around his heart. He grabbed the stair railing to steady himself.

Sitting stunned on the stairs, he stared into space, taking deep breaths and trying not to cry out loud. He held his hands tightly together as if to force himself to have some sense of control. This was the woman he loved with all his being. Sharon was his best friend and lover. There could never be anyone in the world who could mean as much to him. The closeness between them was palpable, something even strangers would remark upon after spending a short time with them.

It took a moment, but eventually, the anger moved in.

Who the hell is this guy, and what's he doing in my bed with my wife? I can't just walk away from this. Christ, what am I supposed to do?

Then he heard talking coming from the bedroom.

Now is the time to walk in, he thought.

It was one of the hardest things he'd ever done. He unclenched his hands, stood up, and pushed the door open.

He walked into the middle of the room and just stared silently at his wife. Sharon sat with the covers tucked under her armpits. She had the grace to lower her eyes and then raise her hands to cover her face, too shocked to react in any other way. But Tim still saw the pain in her eyes.

Without saying a word, he turned and walked out of the room. Holding the banister, he ran down the stairs and went into the library. For the second time that day, his hands were shaking. He poured himself a scotch, even though it was only nine thirty, and sank into his chair. After about ten minutes, he heard the front door slam. Then a car started and drove away.

One moment Tim wanted to hide from Sharon. The next he found himself staring at the door waiting for her to come in. He jumped up from his chair to walk to the door and confront her but then returned to his seat and sat back down.

She made the decision for him by walking into the library, dressed in a pair of hastily thrown-on sweats and a T-shirt. Her whole body was slumped in pure anguish. When she saw his drink, she went to the bar and poured herself one as well. She came over to sit close to him, but he quickly moved away. He was frightened to be near her. He would be unable to breathe if she sat too close.

Sharon stayed seated, sadly watching Tim move away from her. He sat down again in another chair, and she noticed his whole body was tight and tense. He almost looked as if he could break the glass he was holding with his bare hands. She was frightened, but even more so she felt such shame and sorrow, something she had never experienced this strongly before. His movement away from her and the silence in the room were more than she could bear.

"Tim…please talk to me," Sharon pleaded. She gripped her now unwanted glass of scotch with trembling hands and waited. If only he would say something. Anything. His silence frightened her.

But Tim was completely incapable of saying anything. He could only hear nonsensical screaming inside his head. He could not even look at her. Instead, he stared at the wall of books without actually seeing them.

Sharon finally spoke. Tim did not hear all she said, but a few words got through. His first few hits at his scotch were gulps—big ones. By the time he was halfway finished with his second scotch, more of what she was saying got through to him. It helped that she kept saying the same things over and over, trying desperately to get him to listen to her.

"Please don't hate me. Please don't hate me," she said. He saw the pain in her eyes and the tears running down her face but could not reconcile that with the image of her in bed with another man.

She knew that her betrayal was unforgivable, but there was also love in her eyes. Tim had seen this love many times in the past, in many moments in the years they had been together. He remembered the day he asked her to marry him. He had seen that look of love in her eyes then. How in the world was this disaster possible?

After finishing his second scotch, Tim realized he could not just sit in silence, but he had no idea what to say. He didn't want to say anything. Talking to Sharon right now was too painful.

He finally stood up and walked out of the room. As he left the room, he stopped at the door, turned to Sharon, and, using all his strength to get the words out, said, "Leave me alone."

He left the house and went back to his shed. He had no idea what he would do there, and he didn't care. He could not be in his house for another second.

Chapter Six

MICHELE ARRIVED HOME TO AN EMPTY HOUSE. SHE WAS never home alone, so this was a wonderful treat for her. With Sam having left for school on the bus early in the morning, long before the accident, she would have the place all to herself for the entire day. Michele decided the perfect start to a day alone would be a cup of hot tea and a chance to browse through a couple of old magazines. She slipped into her most comfortable sweats and slippers and arranged herself on the couch surrounded by her favorite decorating magazines and her tea, which smelled of sweet lemons. Holding the warm teacup in her hands and sniffing in the flavored steam felt absolutely decadent.

After what seemed an awfully short time, Michele's phone started to buzz. Her first reaction was to sigh. She was so comfortable and relaxed that she almost ignored it, trying to make it go away, but since Sam was in school, she still had to see if the call concerned him.

The number on her phone was his school. Her reverie broken, Michele immediately answered the call.

"Ms. Myer, this is Principal Adams calling. I am so sorry to tell you that there has been an accident this morning in the schoolyard. Sam was playing and took a very hard fall from the jungle gym."

Michele, not sure she had heard correctly, stopped her. "Wait, what? What happened?"

The principal kept talking. "We are waiting for an ambulance now. It appears to be some sort of neck injury."

Feeling her heart start to race, Michele interrupted her again. "What are you saying? Is it bad? Why an ambulance? Is this something serious?"

"Yes, I am afraid so."

"Is he going to be okay?"

Principal Adams spoke again. "I really can't give you an answer right now. As soon as the ambulance arrives, I'll call and let you know which hospital they take him to. You should know the school nurse is with him and will ride with him in the ambulance. I need you to stay by your phone. We will be in touch very shortly."

Michele had no idea what to say. She vaguely remembered responding, saying something like, "Of course. Thank you."

Immediately after she hung up, Michele found herself shaking. She went up to her room to grab a pair of shoes, her purse, and her car keys, making sure that she kept the phone with her wherever she went. She threw some extra things in a bag in case Sam would have to spend a night at the hospital.

Michele walked around the house, constantly checking her phone for an agonizing ten minutes, waiting to hear which hospital her son was at. When she received the call, she realized she was unable to get to the hospital since the highway was still closed. Michele paced around the house, checking her watch every few minutes. She walked into the kitchen and then back out to the couch, where her computer was on, watching for the news of the road and whether the police had opened it. It was a terrible wait knowing her little boy was hurt and she could do nothing to get to him. She imagined him being frightened in strange surroundings and wondering where she was. Michele felt relieved that the school nurse was with Sam so he had someone with him that he knew. Fortunately, Sam's school was not cut off from the hospital.

An agonizing thirty minutes later, the police opened the highway. Michele flew out of her house and drove as fast as she had ever dared. She gripped the steering wheel in panic while she drove. When she reached the hospital, she pulled into the closest spot she could find. She jumped out, slammed the door, and didn't even bother to lock the car, running to follow the signs to the emergency room. Passing through the doors and entering the emergency room area, she rushed to the front desk. She explained to the receptionist who she was and received directions to the room where she could find her son.

Sam looked so tiny in his bed. It didn't help that he had a huge brace wrapped around his head and neck, but he was conscious, and when he saw his mother, his smile radiated through to his eyes.

Sam immediately called out to Michele, "Mommy, Mommy, you're here!"

Michele was so happy to see Sam smile that she did not realize, at first, that he was not reaching for her in any way. He was completely still in the bed. When she noticed his stillness, even without speaking to a doctor, her heart froze as she began to comprehend the implications of his fall. Michele kept stroking his face and giving him little kisses. She spoke quietly to him, with a confidence she didn't feel, telling him everything was going to be okay.

"Buddy, I'll be right back, okay? I just want to check with whoever is in charge. I'll be right back." She then tore herself away from his bedside to talk to one of the doctors.

Michele went straight to the nurse's station to ask for the doctor who was treating her son. Doctor Mary Silk was standing at the station, so she introduced herself as the attending physician. She took Michele to the waiting area and tried to explain the injury and the repercussions.

"It appears that Sam fell on his neck and broke it in several places. We've stabilized him and will need to wait to see the lasting damage. We're going to keep him here in the ICU where we can monitor him carefully."

Michele had only one question: Would he ever be able to move again? But she didn't have the strength to ask. She found herself just staring at the doctor and then back at the door to Sam's room. Crossing her arms over her chest as if to protect herself from something she did not want to hear and feeling like she couldn't articulate any other questions while her mind was racing, she gave up for the moment and simply nodded to the doctor.

Back in Sam's room, Michele pulled up a chair next to his bed, gave him her biggest smile, and said, "Hey there, handsome!"

Hours later, in the middle of the night, another doctor came in to check on Sam. This doctor touched Sam's face to let him know he was there. After listening to his chest, he gently picked up Sam's hand and gave it a squeeze to see if there was any reaction, but there was none. The doctor told Sam and Michelle that the MRI was open and available, and they had booked it for Sam, even though it was late at night.

Walking through the brightly lit corridors in the middle of the night was surreal. Everything was quiet, except for the constant beeping that exists in any hospital.

Michele clasped her hands in prayer while Sam was in the MRI machine. It had been a long time since she had prayed—her life had been busy, and she and Sam had allowed prayer time to lapse. Now, when disaster struck, her religion came pouring back. Michele's prayer was minimal: "Please God, *please God*, let him be okay."

After the MRI, Sam went back to the ICU. Michele pushed two chairs together in his room to form some semblance of a bed. While she lay there trying to get some sleep, she kept rubbing her eyes, trying not to panic and fall apart. She fell in and out of a doze until the sun woke her in the morning.

Dr. Silk arrived early the next morning. She sat down to talk to Michele out in the hallway and was prepared to answer her questions. She explained, "Sam has some small fractures in his neck, but also one large one."

The doctor pulled out the pictures to show Michele the fractures. She traced each of the gray areas on the X-rays with her fingers so Michele could see exactly where they were.

"He doesn't seem to have any feeling in his limbs or in any part of his body below his neck. He's young, and that works in his favor; however, we really don't know yet if the paralysis is temporary or permanent."

The doctor stopped to give Michele a chance to grasp all the information. Michele was in shock and trying her best to absorb everything she was hearing. She kept rubbing her face with shaking hands. She felt a huge knot in the pit of her stomach that made it difficult to breathe, much less speak.

After a moment, the doctor resumed.

"Some of the paralysis may disappear in one area but stay in others, so we would like to move Sam to our neurology ward and keep him there for more tests by our specialists."

Again, the doctor stopped and asked Michele, "Do you have any questions so far?"

Michele just shook her head, trying to get her mind around all the information.

The doctor continued. "After that, we would like to move him to a facility that specializes in paralysis victims, someplace where the staff is accustomed to dealing with these kinds of injuries."

Michele was stunned. Again, she felt the knot in her stomach and realized she was holding her breath. After taking a gulp of air, she nodded to the doctor. She was still having difficulty speaking.

The doctor gently touched Michele's arm and said, "Look, I know this is a lot and very scary, but he is in very good hands. We will do the very best we can for him."

She then excused herself, telling Michele to contact her immediately if she thought of any questions. Michele sat still for a moment, and then she gripped the arms of the chair to rise. Her legs were shaking, and she was not sure if she had the strength to stay on her feet. From there, she went straight to the restroom.

She leaned on the sink and stared at herself in the mirror. What she saw terrified her. Her face was pale, and her mouth was a tight slit. When she looked into her eyes, they began to tear up. At that point, she turned on the sink and started splashing cold water onto her face. She kept at it for two or three minutes, trying to get some degree of self-control. She did not dare to walk into Sam's room looking like a ghost woman.

When she felt she had a modicum of control, she grabbed several paper towels and vigorously rubbed her face dry. The roughness of the towels gave her face a rose-colored tint, which helped her look a little better.

As she started back to Sam's room, she began to think of his future. She couldn't imagine not seeing this beautiful child running around on the farm and learning all his daily chores. Michele felt her mind racing, but she knew the most important thing was to pull herself together and keep going. This was not the time for her to be indecisive. Nor was it the time for her to indulge herself and allow her fears to delay any efforts to improve Sam's situation.

When she reached Sam's room, she forced herself to adopt a casual expression. Gripping her purse tightly under her arm, she pushed against the door carefully so as not to slam it open. She walked over to give Sam a kiss and a smile, but her mind was on what actions she needed to take. She would talk to specialists, move Sam to another facility, anything to care for her sweet boy, while taking everything one day at a time.

Chapter Seven

JEFF WAS ANNOYED AT NOT BEING ABLE TO GET TO WORK. After he called in to alert the store he could not get in today, he was even more bothered by the change to his routine. The manager at his company was not the nicest of individuals and would probably make him work on Saturday to make up for the lost time.

Jeff loved his weekends alone with Dell. The weekends were their special time together; spending the whole day talking, laughing, and sometimes just quietly hanging out was heaven. They often spent hours at the local plant store. He and Dell were very careful with their money, but they agreed on their biggest splurge: flowers for their garden. In fact, they loved to putter around, planting and meticulously pruning so that each year the garden grew more beautiful.

Jeff and Dell had had many conversations about what their lives would be like once Jeff retired. Just last night after dinner they pulled out a large piece of paper and began to design new sections of their yard. They both looked forward to spending days in the garden or in the library studying ways to improve their garden. Jeff adored Dell and delighted in glancing over to see her face smudged with dirt. Although her skin had toughened from the sun, Jeff thought she was beautiful. After raising their family, they could work side by side for hours without speaking, in complete joy and comfort.

After some time to think on the drive home, Jeff started to get excited knowing he had a day off. He and Dell could have a lovely lunch outside and start planning what to do with the pots they had bought last weekend.

Maybe it's time to start growing herbs, he thought. Once retired, Jeff thought he might enjoy cooking more. He was a very fit sixty-five-year-old, partially through good genes but also because he liked to eat properly. Dell made the most delicious meals for him to take to work. After his retirement, perhaps he could join her in the kitchen and help prepare the many meals they would enjoy together.

He smiled while driving, imagining himself joining Dell in the kitchen. They could put on some great music, pour each other cocktails, and dance around each other while putting together some world-class cuisine! He even imagined himself learning how to make homemade pasta.

As he pulled into his driveway, he could not wait to see Dell's reaction to having him home for the day. Walking into the house, Jeff yelled her name even before he closed the front door.

"Dell! Dell, yoohoo! We have a day to enjoy! Dell? Where are you, woman?"

There was no answer. *Well,* he thought, *she must be upstairs.*

"Dell! Dell!"

Jeff walked upstairs to their room, fully expecting to see the surprise on Dell's face. He was grinning like a schoolboy thinking of all the fun they would have today. Walking past the bed to the bathroom, Jeff felt his foot bang against something on the floor.

Looking down to see what he had hit, Jeff's chest lurched.

He saw Dell lying crumpled on the floor. Her one arm was underneath her at an odd angle and the other stretched out on the floor, as if she had simply collapsed in a pile.

"Oh my God! *Dell*."

When Jeff grabbed her shoulders and felt her dead weight, he knew she was gone. Shock coursed through his system.

He lifted her close to his chest as if this could somehow change what had happened. Holding her in his arms, he was horrified that he had not been home when she needed him the most. Moments passed as he held her, rocking her in his arms. He gasped, feeling an intense pain in his chest. Then he gently placed her body on the floor, tenderly touched her face, and sobbed.

After what seemed like ages, a stunned Jeff finally made the call to 911. It seemed an endless number of people came tromping through his home, all with questions. For someone who wanted to be under the radar, he had become the most important person in the room.

The emergency crew were very respectful as they went about the task of lifting Dell and placing her body on the gurney. One of the EMTs stayed in the bedroom with Jeff while the others carried Dell down the stairs and out into the waiting ambulance. When the EMT saw they were ready to go, he once again offered his condolences, gave his name to Jeff, and asked if there was anything he could do for him before he left. Jeff just looked at him and shook his head.

When the house finally emptied, Jeff had a moment to sit, and although he thought his heart could stand no more pain, he realized he had one more duty to perform: He had to call his son and daughter.

He and Dell had a very old-fashioned marriage. She was the one who raised the children and the one who made the time he spent with them mean something. Jeff enjoyed his children but was not the central person in their lives.

His hands shook uncontrollably as he held his phone. This was not going to be easy.

Chapter Eight

TIM WOKE AFTER A NIGHT OF ALMOST NO SLEEP AND
sat up, feeling distraught and drained. Sitting on the edge of
the bed and rubbing his face, he tried to plan what he was
going to do that day. Standing up, he threw the covers over the
bed and reluctantly went into his bedroom, *their* bedroom, to
shower and get dressed. Fortunately, Sharon was somewhere
else in the house, and he did not have to face her. He dressed
as quickly as he could, went straight out to his car, and drove
to work.

After working at his desk for several hours, he could no
longer sit in his office. He needed a distraction, something to
hopefully take his mind off the ache in his heart. At noon, Tim
walked the four blocks to his usual lunch spot, the Palm, where
he sat at the bar and tried to work up an appetite.

The place was packed, as usual, and the noise from waiters
rushing in and out of the kitchen and conversations at every
table was deafening. Tim ordered the daily special, not even
knowing what it was. When it arrived, he pushed the crab

cake around and managed to eat a small portion of the apples sliced into the dish. This was one of his favorite meals, one of the restaurant's best, but he could not force himself to eat. He felt like he had a crater in his stomach.

While sitting at the bar, he looked in the mirror behind the bartender. He wasn't sure he recognized himself. He looked the same, but his eyes had a hollow, empty look. He quickly looked away, not liking what he saw. Even the bartender must have noticed something because he didn't try to engage Tim in their usual banter. Tim eventually finished his club soda and left behind most of his entrée.

As always, he walked back from lunch, passing by St. Matthew's Cathedral. Although he was raised a Catholic, he had lapsed and had not been inside a church in years. Looking up at the spires and the giant doors, Tim felt himself pulled inside. The quiet and coolness of the cathedral offered a small measure of solace.

After sitting in a pew for some time, Tim knelt and buried his face in his hands. When he looked up again, surrounded by the colors from the stained-glass windows and the flickering of the candles, he saw a priest head for the confessional. His desperation for an answer to a question he did not know how to frame propelled him inside. Once there, his Catholic memory kicked in.

"Forgive me, Father, for I have sinned," he began. "It has been many years since my last confession."

The priest's voice was soft but very kind. "Welcome back," he said.

Tim struggled. "I don't know where to begin. I…I came home unexpectedly yesterday and found my wife in bed with a stranger. I'm desperate. I'm at a complete loss. I don't know how to even feel. I don't know what to do."

Tim choked back a sob. He was trying so hard not to cry. He rubbed his hands over his face, trying to continue.

When he finally regained some measure of control, he said, "Please tell me what to do."

While listening to Tim through the grate, Father O'Hara slumped in his seat. He could feel the pain coming from the man as he heard him speak. He raised his hand toward the partition as if he could touch the man on the other side but then dropped it as he realized it was a useless gesture.

The priest replied, "I am so sorry for your pain. What a horrible, gut-wrenching situation. I've heard this before, yet I am always surprised at the enormous sorrow and sense of loss it can cause."

The priest moved slightly closer to Tim, as if to offer physical support, despite the barrier between them.

"I would love to help you, but for the moment, you need to give yourself some time. The pain will ease, and you will start to feel better."

The priest could sense the disbelief through the caged partition.

"I always tell the people involved to talk to one another as often as they can. I tell them to remember their vows. I'm sure you remember the part about 'for better or for worse.' This is, for you both, the worse. You must give yourself some time."

"I don't know if I have the strength to give any time to this," Tim replied. As he spoke, he leaned forward and grasped the edge of the screen. Talking about this made it real. Tim was terrified to say it, but he had to.

"Maybe I should just go home and move out. I have loved this woman with my whole heart and soul. She has been my best friend and soulmate for twenty-four years. We never argue, and we enjoy each other's company immensely. Some evenings we spent hours over dinner, just talking about everything under the sun. I thought she felt the same way about me, but now I just don't know."

Tim closed his eyes, trying to listen to what the priest had to say. When he released his grip on the screen, he realized his knees were starting to shake. The adrenaline that had been coursing through his system was taking its toll. He leaned back from the kneeler and tried to sit down.

"I understand your feelings," the priest answered with tenderness. "Not just of loss and betrayal but of confusion as well. I would counsel you, under these extreme conditions, to make no decisions right away."

Once again, the priest paused, as if to gather his thoughts.

"Please give this some time and prayer. God can be your confidant, and you will be amazed at how comforting the communication between you and God can be. Are you willing to give God, and time, a try?"

Tim sat frozen in his seat. Taking a deep breath, he ran his hands through his hair, trying to think. What the priest said was true. If he was honest with himself, he was desperately hoping that this whole thing could somehow be fixed or explained. Or maybe time could be turned back so it never happened? Was there even an explanation that could make him feel better? Tim searched for anything that would help him resolve the crisis, but there was nothing for him to find, nothing that he could see.

Opening his eyes, he finally responded. "Yes, Father, I will give it some time. I don't know how this will end, but I will give it a try. Thank you very much for talking with me. I am not sure I feel any *better*, but I'm somewhat calmer."

"Bless you, my son. I will say prayers for you and your wife. And you are always welcome to come and speak with me. I am

Father O'Hara, and you can call and set up an appointment, or you can just come back to the confessional. I am always here on the same days at the same times. Bless you in the name of the Father, Son, and Holy Ghost."

After Tim left the confessional, he lingered in the back of the cathedral. In the space lit only by candlelight, the smell of incense, the beauty of the saints depicted in mosaics, and the rows upon rows of polished wooden pews gave him a small measure of peace.

Tim reluctantly left the church and went back to his office, where he just stared out the window. The sun was shining brightly, and he normally loved to see it reflect off the tall building's windows, but not today. He clearly was not going to get any work done. After a short while, he went to the garage to get his car. Not knowing what to do, he started the car and began his normal drive home.

As the minutes passed, Tim began counting highway markers to stop the spinning in his head. About ten miles into the trip, he finally felt himself calming and starting to breathe normally. Only then would his brain allow him to begin to think.

What do I do now? If I go home to pack up and leave, I will lose the only person I've ever loved. Where would I even go? But if I stay, nothing will ever be the same.

For a moment, he thought he should load all his belongings into his car, drive away, and never return. But the thought of not seeing her was so painful that it once again felt like a clamp on his heart.

When he arrived home, he turned off the motor and just sat in his car, staring at his front door. He loved this house, and looking over his garden, he felt tremendous pride in the beauty of his home. It was large and older, with a bright-red door and white bricks. Shiny black shutters surrounded all the windows.

White and red geraniums lined the front walkway, interspersed with elegant wrought-iron chairs. The place appeared to have such warmth, especially when the sun lit up the front.

Taking a deep breath, Tim forced himself out of his car and into the house, where he changed his clothes and went back to his shed. Dinner was something he threw together and ate standing at the kitchen sink. He had almost no appetite anyway.

Sharon was tempted to try to speak with Tim, but she was afraid that he would just push her away. She kept to herself, quietly reading in the living room. She was not interested in dinner, so she made herself a hot tea and some toast. She was hoping that his coming home meant something positive, but the air in the house felt heavy.

The next day, before the sun came up, Tim filled a travel mug with coffee and got on the highway into the city. He spent the day at his office, fielding phone calls, reading emails, and going to lunch, trying to perform as if nothing had happened.

Around one o'clock, he tried getting out of the office and walked by the cathedral again, but this time he couldn't make himself go in. He needed to move, so he wandered around the city, not really seeing anything.

As he walked the city streets, he could not help noticing couples walking together. He found himself wondering about their lives. *How are they together? Are they happy? Do they have any answers for me?*

After another miserable day, he got back into his car, wondering what to do. Because he could not make up his mind, he began his normal route home, but as he was driving, his eyes began to tear up again. He had to use all his self-control just so he could continue.

Tim's tortured questions played endlessly until he pulled into his driveway. There were no answers.

Sharon was at the doorway when Tim arrived home. After spending her morning making plans for the evening, she launched herself into action.

Walking through the market, feeling frightened, Sharon started rapidly grabbing all the items she would need to make this weekend a good one, or at least as good as she could. She reached for a block of taleggio cheese and a box of rice crackers. Pâté, prosciutto, and massive steaks for the grill filled her cart.

After she finished her shopping, Sharon dove through her closet, looking for the right outfit. It had to look soft and lovely, something to catch his eye so he could see she was trying. Pulling out a flowery sundress and putting on a pair of slender sandals, she tied her hair into a long ponytail with soft tendrils loose at the side. She looked beautiful, and he noticed.

At the front door, she tried to look nonchalant while holding a glass of wine for him, but her heart was racing. She knew her marriage could end right now.

"It is a Meursault, your favorite. Please, please, come to the patio with me. We can talk. You can yell. Anything you want. Just please let me know what you're thinking."

Tentatively, she placed the glass in his hand. Then she pushed open the door to their home, trying to get him to come inside to a place that used to feel so safe and warm for them both.

Speaking in a wavering, soft voice, Sharon said, "I am so, so sorry. I did something horrible, the worst thing I've ever done in my life, but I can't lose you. Please, *please* come and talk to me."

Tim couldn't help but follow Sharon through the house to the patio, where she'd set the table with his favorite cheese and crackers. She sat in the chair across from him, not too close, but not too far away, having learned that lesson from the library the morning before.

Sitting silently, Sharon hoped he would start the conversation. If they could talk, she thought, they might have a chance.

Tim managed to ask quietly, "Why?"

But before Sharon could answer, he asked more loudly, "*Who?*"

Looking into Tim's eyes, Sharon decided that "who" was the easier first answer.

"It really doesn't matter. He was a person of absolutely no consequence."

Hoping that Tim would not notice her shaking hands, she said, "I don't mean to minimize your question, but that person meant nothing to me. It's important to me that you understand that."

Looking straight into Tim's eyes, she said, "I desperately want you to know that you are the only person I have ever loved. It was just a stupid—"

Tim looked at her suspiciously, wondering how Sharon could be involved in such an intimate manner with someone she had no feelings for whatsoever. He wasn't ready to let that idea go.

"Why?" he asked. "I thought we were so happy."

Sharon stiffened in her chair. "Yes, we were very happy! I loved you and *do* love you with all my heart. This had nothing to do with that."

"What is that supposed to mean?" Tim asked in anger. "It doesn't even make sense! You can't behave like that and say it meant nothing."

Sharon cast down her eyes and said softly, "We were happy when we were together, but a lot of the time I was so lonely here. The days were so long, and I felt like my life was drifting past me and I had no control."

With her eyes tearing up, she continued. "I wanted to have

some fun. You were gone so much of the time, and your life during the day had nothing to do with me."

Hesitating for a moment to gather her thoughts, she reached for her wine. "When we're together, we're so happy. When you're gone, I don't exist for you. Then I start to feel like I don't exist at all. Your interest in me was only when we were together." Without taking a single sip of her wine, she placed it back on the table. "So I became involved with someone who made me exist."

Tim was anxious to get up and move, but the look on Sharon's face made him stay on the patio. He got up and started pacing.

"How long?"

"A year…maybe a year…and a half," she answered slowly and in a very quiet voice.

He was shaken to his very core. *How could this have happened for all this time without my ever guessing or questioning?* Was there something else he didn't know about her? Tim had to lower his eyes at the thought. All the emotions were taking their toll. His body started to sag, and he put his hands on the table for support. He had no energy left.

A numbness descended over him, and he dropped back into his seat. Sharon, sensing his anguish, stepped in to direct the conversation.

With tears starting to run down her face, she said, "I'm so sorry. I did something horribly wrong. But the most important thing to me is that I don't lose you. Will you please give us some time to try to work things out? I'll see a therapist. I'll look for someone tomorrow. I love you, and I don't want to lose you. Please, can we try?"

Using a paper napkin to wipe her eyes, she watched Tim's face, hoping to see something to cling to. Sharon desperately prayed Tim would give her a chance to repair the marriage. She thought it best if she didn't mention that she had ended her relationship with the other man, thinking it would just refresh the anguish she saw in Tim's eyes.

Tim noticed how frightened Sharon's voice was and saw her hands shaking. He thought she was sincere, but how would he know? He could not make a choice tonight.

They moved inside to eat dinner, but the meal was very quiet and strained. Tim decided he would sleep again in the guest room. He was still so very confused, angry, and hurt. He could not see a way that they could possibly work this out. Before falling into another night of restless sleep, Tim remembered Father O'Hara's pleas to take some time.

In the morning, he again decided no decision was the best decision. It was a Saturday, and it looked beautiful outside.

He got out of bed and dressed in his most comfortable slacks and T-shirt, electing to not bother with any shoes. He thought he would bury himself in the newspapers and all the little chores that accumulate around the house.

Breakfast was cordial, but unlike the past, when mornings together meant sharing stories from the newspaper and quietly reading with that inexplicable connection one feels with someone simply by being in the same room, today two silent strangers shared a meal.

During the day, Tim spent his time outside on the property or in his shed, just to be away from Sharon. Rumbling around, he moved old cans and broken screens to the front door. Manual labor helped him to hold himself together. After several hours, he got his wheelbarrow and started hauling the trash out to the driveway. By nighttime he was tired, so he went into the kitchen and grabbed a microwave pizza and a beer. Then he went into the library and closed the doors.

Once again, he slept in the guest room. He could not bear the thought of being in that bed. He knew he had more questions, but he needed time to figure out what they were. How else could he understand what happened? If he could not understand the why, then there was absolutely no chance to move forward. He immediately recognized that for him even thinking of reconciliation, he had made some sort of decision. Crawling under the covers and feeling completely drained, he turned out the lights, knowing he did not have the strength or the desire to read. Before falling asleep, Tim looked out his window at the heavens and pleaded, "Please help me."

Meanwhile, Sharon slept on her side of their bed holding Tim's pillow. She, too, stared out the windows until the tears rolled down the sides of her face and dampened the sheets. She desperately wanted to go into the guest room and crawl into bed with Tim, but she didn't have the nerve, so she lay in her bed feeling as lonely as she ever had.

Sunday morning started early. Sharon was already up and beautifully dressed, making Tim's favorite breakfast and setting it all up on the patio. She was marginally hopeful for a reconciliation since Tim had not left their home. She desperately wanted to stay married and was convinced they could be happy again.

Sharon smiled at Tim when he walked into the kitchen.

"Good morning, my love. I have all your favorites, so why don't we just enjoy the morning?"

Tim nodded and took his place at the table. This morning Sharon sat a little closer to him than the day before, and Tim did not move away. He felt the warm summer breeze and the quiet of the country and realized, *No decision today.*

Although his heart was shattered, the normalcy of the moment relaxed him somewhat, and he felt comforted by Sharon's presence.

Chapter Nine

MICHELE TOOK A FEW HOURS TO GO HOME, AFTER MUCH urging by the doctors. After walking through the front door, she stopped for a moment and leaned back against the doorjamb. Even with the sun shining into the living room, her beautiful house just felt hollow and empty. She forced herself up the stairs and managed a shower, clean clothes, and a few bites of food. Before heading back to the hospital, she went into Sam's room and gathered up some of his favorite toys and books.

Picking through all the toys that accumulate in any child's room, she angrily pushed away any that would require him to move. That meant no Game Boy, Legos, or even some of his collection of Matchbox cars. She settled on books, videos, and music on her laptop, and some soft plush toys. She realized he must be so frightened that anything to get his mind off where he was and the equipment he was wearing would be good for him.

When Michele reached the hospital, Sam was wide awake and had a huge smile on his face. He was always the happiest child!

After an hour of reading *Charlotte's Web*, Michele told Sam she needed to use the restroom and that she would be back very shortly.

Out in the hall, she managed to catch Dr. Silk between patients.

"I'm sorry. Do you have a moment? I was wondering, where do we go from here?" she asked.

Dr. Silk looked at Michele kindly and responded, "Walk with me so we can talk."

They headed down the hospital corridor, passing rolling beds, equipment, and multiple computer outlets.

"The very best would be to get Sam to a facility specializing in paralysis. There, they will be able to assess if there is any chance of partial or full recovery. They will also begin a series of physical therapy sessions that will keep his muscles from deteriorating."

Reaching into her pocket to get out a pen and a notepad, she started writing.

"I can recommend several facilities. Why don't you try to visit them this afternoon or tomorrow? We will take very good care of Sam while you are gone."

The doctor had reached her next patient's room and needed to go in, but she reiterated to Michele, "Investigating some of the places will give you a feeling of forward movement. Please go soon."

Michele girded herself for what she needed to do. She had no idea what to expect, and after lunch with Sam, off she went.

Of the two facilities that were anywhere near where Michele lived, one was horrible. As she wandered through the building, she was appalled by the condition. The hall floors were grimy, and the rooms were merely walls placed between beds, with linoleum floors and very few windows.

The other place was downright depressing—walls without pictures, and equipment parked in the hallways. As she walked through the hallways, she could not help but look into some of the rooms where the doors were open. Inside, she saw people sitting in wheelchairs, staring at their televisions.

Well, she thought, *depressing can be handled if you change the arena once you get there.*

Michele needed to speak to her employer about the situation. It would be a difficult conversation, but Sam came first. Despite needing the income, she had no intention of allowing anyone to change her priorities.

Sitting in her kitchen looking out to the back of the house, Michele pulled up her office number, then put down the phone, only to pick it up again. It was difficult to campaign for herself to her supervisor, but it was in Sam's best interest.

She finally pushed the green button, and the call went through. In a matter of minutes, her supervisor told her, "Please take the time you need. I am so sorry to hear about your little boy. All of us here at the magazine will be thrilled to do whatever we can to make this easier for you. Just let us know what you need."

Releasing her death grip on her phone, Michele expressed her gratitude and promised to keep in touch and to continue to do whatever she could from home.

Then Michele went up to Sam's room and dug through all his drawers. She pulled T-shirts and shorts out and put them on his bed. These would be easy to dress him in. She hated seeing him in pajamas all day.

She pulled out her laptop and ordered several knickknacks to place around Sam's room. Throwing herself into improving and decorating Sam's room at the facility allowed her to feel involved in his recovery.

On the day of the move, Michele and Sam waited outside the hospital for the ambulance to pull up. Sam was curious about moving to a new place. He asked many times, "Mom, where is this place? Can I go outside there? Are there other kids there? What is the food like?"

Michele did her best to answer his questions honestly. Sam was such a happy and smart little guy, he instinctively knew all Michele's changes were for his benefit. This is not to say he did not have his moments. Inside the ambulance, he settled down and got very quiet. Michele followed in her car, worrying about him the entire time they were separated.

When they first arrived at the new facility, his eyes were very large, and at times he got a little teary looking around. He had quite a few questions for her. The first one was "Mommy, will you be staying here with me?"

Michele crumpled inside and took a deep breath to answer him.

"No, darling," she said quietly. "I can't sleep here with you. But I'll come every day. I promise."

That night she helped him with his dinner, after which she could see his exhaustion. The move had taken a lot of his energy. Rubbing his head, she tucked him into bed. After a good long kiss and an "I love you," she told him to sleep well and that she would be back early the next morning.

As she left his room, her eyes filled with tears she could not let him see.

Every morning when she got to the facility, she walked through the dark hallways looking at the floor, not wanting to ever again see into any of the other rooms. She hurried to get to Sam's room, where she immediately opened the curtains to let the daylight in.

Michele watched him carefully to ensure he was adjusting

well to his new surroundings and his new reality of not being able to run and play as he had before. Sam fussed on occasion, but Michele and Sam's nurses did their best to keep his mind, if not his body, entertained. As odd as it may have seemed, the paralysis was a blessing, since he was unable to feel any of the pain from his accident. His ready smile made the transition that much easier for Michele.

On Michele's first morning after moving Sam, she got up very early so she could have breakfast with him. Before leaving the house, she stepped outside her back door with her coffee. The flowers were blooming, and the birds were chirping. Even the air smelled good, just like so many other mornings. It was all so routine, except Sam was not there. It was a tough adjustment for them both, but Michele was intent on doing what was best for her son.

Sam's physical therapist came daily and very gently moved Sam's arms and legs to keep his circulation going. The therapist was a lovely young woman named Cathy, and Sam loved to see her just for the company and for the latest magical story she fascinated him with each session.

Michele had a rough time going home at night, but Sam seemed to settle into his room. When she got home, she found herself wandering around without much purpose. She ended up putting together something to eat, but it just didn't feel right having dinner by herself. At first she kept the television on to make some noise, but after a while it was just that: noise.

She finished her dinner in record time and looked around the kitchen. She saw just the sad single dish and fork looking lonely sitting in the sink. It was not even enough to run the dishwasher. She placed her head in her hands and allowed herself a few quiet tears, terrified at what was to come. She wondered how she would handle things when it was time for Sam to come home. However, she could not imagine Sam living in a hospital room for very long. She missed him so much and missed all their daily routines. And no one should have to live in such a sterile setting.

After meeting with several specialists, Michele learned it would be at least four weeks before Sam could come home. She noted the date on the calendar in the kitchen. It was something that she would mark off each and every day. She spent that time deciding how to configure her home to accommodate Sam's condition.

This was a very difficult period for her. Her days consisted of trips to and from the facility and a few hours at night working. As she drove each morning, she thought of what to do that day to occupy Sam. Each day was a little different—reading, watching TV, and even dancing in the room, trying her best to keep Sam entertained.

Michele realized that she and Sam were, in a sense, a dynamic duo. They had arranged a life for themselves that did not involve many other people. Michele was very private. Having grown up on the farm where she and Sam lived, she was accustomed to spending a great deal of time alone. She had no siblings, and the rural nature of the area meant there were no children who could just come over to play. A large part of her day as a child included daily chores, which she took very seriously. It was the same for Sam. After he finished all his chores, he had time for homework, reading, and just playing outside—climbing trees, making a fort, chasing frogs.

When she first learned of her pregnancy, she had already been living on her own for several years. Her parents died in a car accident when she was only twenty-one years old. The car in which they were driving was coming over a rise, and they were unable to see a large tractor in front of them. There were no shoulders and no way to stop in time.

Michele grieved for her parents alone. Though she was lonely, she did not have to leave her home, so she did not have to start over someplace new. She attended a few church services and even went to one session of a group for people who had lost family members. It was not for her. The group meeting left her feeling more stressed than comforted. She stopped attending and forced herself to focus on her future and the present.

Except for the farm and a very small amount of cash, she was on her own. Michele found employment quickly with a magazine company, doing work she enjoyed. After a brief relationship with Sam's father, which did not end well, she decided that focusing on the farm and her little boy was the life for her.

Up until now, she and Sam had had an idyllic existence. On Saturdays, they planned out their day at breakfast. She and Sam ate a large meal with eggs and toast and sometimes smoothies for them both. With *The Washington Post* open on the table, they looked up all the activities that were going on in the city. They planned everything, from a visit to the zoo or a museum to what they would have for dinner and what movie they would see on television that night. During the week, school, work, and maintaining the farm were enough to keep them both fully occupied. Now, with the accident, the change to their lives would be drastic.

Michele found an excellent lawyer, recommended to her by one of the nurses at the hospital, and talked to him on the phone often. Robert soon became a source of comfort. He had a calm yet confident manner and gave her examples of many cases similar to hers. He explained the laws governing negligence and how they worked.

One afternoon, while Sam was working with Cathy, Robert

told her, "Michele, I don't think I will have any problems getting the manufacturer of the swing set to agree to settle this matter without any court time. I have dealt with their in-house counsel before, and very rarely have I been unable to come to a satisfactory conclusion."

He arranged for a settlement that would help pay for all the changes needed for someone in a wheelchair. The lawyer negotiated with the in-house counsel, who had dealt with Robert before and had great respect for his talent and honesty. The office sent him a check within the week.

Michele wandered through her house to see what kind of accommodations she could make to adjust for Sam's new lifestyle. The first change would be making her dining room into Sam's bedroom so he wouldn't need to use the stairs. Despite feeling guardedly optimistic, she looked at what changes she could make to the house in case Sam remained paralyzed for life.

The doctors had given Michele their best guess on how much progress she could expect for Sam's paralysis. They were not optimistic that he would be able to walk again. Michele realized her life had changed forever. Whatever dreams she'd had for her and Sam were now gone. Having a disabled child was a frightening amount of responsibility, and the thought of all she needed to change kept her awake at night. What would it be like if she needed to run out to the store? What if there was a fire in the house? What would it be like to keep him entertained since she obviously could not send him outside to play? There was so much she would need to learn. When Michele lost her parents, the responsibility was almost overwhelming. But she managed to pull herself together and learn all she needed to move forward.

Michele stopped herself mid-thought.

"Stop! Just stop it. Get yourself into gear!" she said to herself. "This is a transition. A tough one, but still a transition. You can do this. You have to do this. It is for Sam."

Opening the front door, she stepped outside. With a deep breath, she took in the beauty of her surroundings. It had such a calming effect that she began to regain some of her composure.

Michele walked around the property. She saw so many of the projects that she and Sam had done together. She wandered over to his swing set and started pushing the swing.

Watching it sway back and forth, she thought, *I wonder if he will be able to sit in the swing. He used to go so high sometimes it scared me.*

She looked around the farm, trying to think which activities might be out of the question for the future. All the joy she and Sam had doing chores on the farm would change. Michele had not spent a great deal of time imagining what the future would be like for Sam, but like any parent, she had thought of his career, marriage, and family. Now she had to rethink all of that. It was difficult not knowing what kind of barriers Sam would need to overcome to have anything close to a normal life.

Feeling tears in her eyes, Michele thought, *Why did this have to happen to me?*

Then she immediately felt guilty. *What am I thinking? This is about Sam, not about me! Why did this have to happen to him?*

Michele went back into the house and tried to focus on the change she would need to make. She knew the dining room would be a perfect bedroom and would allow him the whole first floor to roam in a wheelchair during the day.

Michele threw herself into a redecorating frenzy. She pushed the dining table closer to the kitchen and pulled chairs first to one corner and then to another. Anything to make room for Sam's new bedroom. There were large windows, so he could look out and see the farm. Michele pulled the curtains all the way to the edges of the window so Sam would be able to see the small barn toward the back of the house with the mountain rising behind it. From inside the house, the changes of seasons and the variety of wildlife would be on display. A ramp could replace the front stairs, and Michele knew just the right handyman who could extend the front porch so Sam could sit outside in good weather.

Life was taking on a new normal, but frightening, feel.

Three weeks into Sam's physical therapy, Cathy was ecstatic to notice a small twitch in one of Sam's fingers during his session.

"Hey, Sam, did you feel that?" Cathy asked.

"I felt it. It was slight, but I felt it!"

"Way to go!"

Cathy immediately called Michele with the good news, and Michele went home that evening feeling like she'd won the lottery. Her heart finally stopped freezing every time she saw Sam, and two weeks later she was able to move him home.

This was an exciting and frightening day for Michele. She desperately wanted Sam home but was terrified to make any mistakes in his care. Just getting him and his wheelchair into the van was a bit of a challenge. The salesman had taught her how to work the ramp and lock the wheelchair into place. Sam just watched quietly. All he knew was that he was going home.

On the drive there, Michele could tell that Sam was as excited as she was, so she tried to see it all from his perspective. She told Sam about all the changes she had made to the house.

Before she could get very far, Sam started asking questions.

"Do I have a TV in my room? Where's my room?"

Michele told him, "No! You definitely do not have a TV in your room! You should know me better than that!"

They both had a good laugh. Sam said, "I had to give it a try."

Sam continued with the questions, now more serious.

"Will I be able to go outside? Will you still be able to push me in my swing set? Can I still sleep outside in a bedroll on warm nights?"

Michele answered as honestly as she could.

"Sam, I'll try my very best to make sure you can do as much as is reasonably possible. There's no reason I can't push you in your swing, but maybe not right away. Some of the things you are going to want to do…well, we will just have to work together to see if we can make them possible." Looking at him through the rearview mirror, she smiled so he would not see how nervous she was. "It might take some extra planning to sleep outdoors, but we will."

Sam smiled back, thrilled to be going home.

"Just you wait and see. Give me some time to figure out how to set everything up. Just so you know, I've contacted school, and we'll have to see what we can do to get you back. Obviously, there will be some changes. It'll all work out, okay?"

"Okay…but are you sure I can't have a TV in my room?"

This got him one of those mom looks in the rearview mirror, which prompted Sam to stick out his tongue.

Once they got home, Sam started planning their special Saturday night dinner and movie, quickly dropping back into their routine.

As Michele worked in the kitchen getting dinner ready, Sam chattered away. He had seen an ad for the movie *Ferdinand*, which was about a bull who lived in Spain but did not want to be in bullfights. It was a lovely movie, and Michele enjoyed it every bit as much as Sam did. Having him home changed her. His joy gave Michele the confidence she needed, and she knew in her heart she would do anything to ensure his health and happiness.

After Sam moved home, Cathy visited him daily and had

even more magical stories, but she pushed him more to give her some resistance when she moved his arms and legs. The twitching became more pronounced and spread to Sam's other fingers. While holding Sam's hand a week after he came home, Cathy felt him push her own hand with his finger. When she looked at his face, Sam was beaming. That night, Michele, Cathy, and Sam had cake. It was a huge celebration.

Sam did not advance every day, but each week they began to see some progress. Sam's legs were still not cooperating, but each day was a new adventure, and that overshadowed the heavy burden Michele carried.

Michele's mornings began with her getting Sam out of his pajamas and into his clothes. Rain or shine, the drapes were always wide open so Sam could begin his day looking outside. Breakfast was a bit of a challenge, but Michele managed to drink her coffee and feed Sam a big plate of bacon and pancakes.

As soon as they finished breakfast, Michele pulled out Sam's schoolwork. His teacher had sent his books and lesson plans so he could keep up with his class.

Sam smiled and joked his way through math, history, and spelling. He often challenged Michele with his answers, making her laugh. It became their special time each day. After they finished all schoolwork, Michele moved Sam outside on the porch or in front of the TV. She then signed on to her computer and started her workday.

Michele's employer made every effort to accommodate her new schedule. She was a mother herself and felt she could understand a little of what Michele was going through. If she could help in any way, she was happy to do so. Michele was now working part time so she could be with Sam more. Everything took twice as long as before. Just getting Sam dressed each day was a major event. But he was making progress, and that gave her hope.

Chapter Ten

JEFF LOVED HIS CHILDREN, BUT DELL HAD THE STRONgest connection with them. They were uninterested in gardening and seemed to have lives that revolved around their spouses and friends. Jeff remembered hearing Dell on the phone with them having the easiest conversations with much laughter, but when she handed the phone to him, the conversation became more stilted.

Jeff was a quiet person. He found relating to others difficult, except Dell. She was always such a good listener and could converse about everything. How in the world was he going to communicate the terrible news about her?

Late in the afternoon, Jeff made his first call to Joanne, his daughter. She answered on the third ring.

"Hi, Mom! What are you up to today?"

Jeff spoke immediately. "It is Dad calling, Joanne."

"Oh? Hi, Dad. What's up? Why are you calling?"

Jeff took a deep breath. "Joanne, you need to sit down. I have some very bad news. I'm so sorry…I…I don't know how to do this, so I'm just going to say it. I'm so sorry, honey, but Mom passed away this morning."

Jeff could hear a gasp, but he kept going, afraid that if he stopped now, he would be unable to continue.

"I came home unexpectedly this morning and…I'm so sorry. By the time I found her, she had been gone for nearly an hour."

Jeff wanted to say more, but he had no idea what else. His eyes teared up, so he stayed quiet and waited to hear what Joanne had to say. Jeff heard another small gasp on the other end of the line and then sobbing.

When she was able to stop crying, Joanne started asking questions. "What happened? Had she been sick? Couldn't anyone do anything?"

Jeff knew she was trying to sort it all out. He answered her questions as well as he could. Having to give her details was very difficult. He felt like he was reliving those awful moments.

Jeff just kept saying how sorry he was, allowing Joanne time to calm down, and then asked her if he could do any-thing to help with her arrangements to come home. He told her he wanted to talk to her brother before setting a date for the funeral.

After hearing some additional sobs, Jeff was about to hang up when Joanne asked, "Daddy, how are you doing?"

After several seconds of silence, Jeff managed to say, "I don't know. I just don't know. I'll talk to you soon, Joanne. Goodbye, dear."

By the time Jeff dialed his son John's number, his hands were shaking and perspiring. John's wife answered the phone and was also surprised that it was Jeff calling.

"Hi, Dad. This is a pleasant surprise! How are you doing?"

Jeff took a deep breath to steady his voice and said, "I have some bad news to give you all. Is John there, please?"

Jeff's son's deep voice came through the phone in an instant. "Hi, Dad. What's going on?"

With a shaking voice, Jeff said, "John, I am so very sorry, but your mother passed away this morning. No one really knows what happened just yet, but it seems it might have been a heart attack or stroke. Your mother was always so healthy, so this has come as a complete shock."

Jeff was starting to ramble, so he quit talking. A stunned silence met him as John was clearly doing his best to keep his composure. Jeff decided to keep speaking to give his son some time.

"I just finished talking to your sister. She was very upset, but I told her we wouldn't make any plans until I could speak to you. If you'd like, you can call her, and the two of you can figure out the best time for you both to come home. I can make the arrangements for the funeral once you two have had a chance to work out the details. Is that all right with you?"

"Oh my god. Uh, yeah…sure," said John. "I'll call Joanne as soon as we hang up. Dad, how are you? How are you holding up? I know how difficult this must be for you."

Again, Jeff had to fight tears. He gripped the phone tightly.

"I don't know, son. Call me soon, okay? Bye."

After Jeff hung up the phone, he collapsed in his chair, shaking all over. He felt an intense pain in his chest. He wanted nothing to do with dinner.

After some time had passed, Jeff was completely drained. Pulling the blanket and his wife's pillow off the bed, he slept fitfully on the floor where he had found Dell.

Before the end of the next day, John and Joanne had made all their arrangements for themselves and their spouses to go home for the funeral. Since they would be home in two days, Jeff scheduled the wake for the evening they got home and the funeral for the next day. They would have a lot to do in those few days.

John and Joanne and their spouses would stay at the house because a hotel seemed too impersonal. Besides, Dell would not have had it any other way. Jeff would have to man up and fix up the rooms the way Dell would have.

Meeting Dell's standards meant clean linens, bottled water, flowers, and magazines in the rooms. He also would have to fill the refrigerator and make sure there was enough of whatever his adult children needed.

Jeff lowered his head and started to cry. He never realized how well Dell had managed their lives. She made it all seem so easy when she was behind the scenes getting everything done. Jeff missed her more than he'd thought it was possible to miss anyone.

When he pulled himself together, he drove to the grocery store and loaded up the cart. He haphazardly threw in bottled water, breakfast food, snacks, and whatever looked easy to cook on the grill for dinner. By the time the cart was full, Jeff was nearing the end of his endurance.

After paying the bill with shaking hands, he loaded up the car and climbed in. He slipped on his seat belt and started the engine. All he wanted was to go home, yet he dreaded returning to an empty house.

When the family arrived, Jeff found himself immersed in the details of getting them settled. He poured everyone a drink and filled them in on the arrangements he had made.

Although he and Dell were not very good about attending mass, Dell would have wanted a funeral mass officiated by a Jesuit priest. He knew the choir needed time to practice and the printer needed the information, so Jeff chose everything the day after he spoke to his children.

"I hope it's all right that I made these decisions without you," he told them. "Your mother had some favorite hymns, and I tried to choose passages that would honor her as the special person she was."

Joanne and John looked lovingly at their father as his voice cracked almost imperceptibly.

Few people attended the wake because Jeff and Dell had spent most of their lives isolated but very happy in each other's company. The funeral was the same, which made for a more intimate yet lovely service, blessed by the most beautiful flowers, many from Jeff and Dell's garden.

It was a beautiful summer day. Jeff strode into the church behind Dell's casket. Before sitting down, he reached out and laid his hand on it. As he sat down, his body slumped, so he started fidgeting with the program, trying to find something to do with his hands. Joanne reached over and put her hand over his, a gesture that touched his heart.

After the funeral and the burial, the family returned to the house. Jeff retired to the isolation of his bedroom. He sat in his chair facing the garden, as he couldn't bear looking at their bed, and lost himself in thought. A numbness descended over him, and the "now what" scenarios began to roam through his mind. He had never contemplated what life would be like without his wife. He could scarcely believe he would never see or talk to her again. All the while he could hear his children and their spouses talking in the living room. Listening to them got him thinking of all the conversations he and Dell had had with the children in that same room. The enormity of what he had lost hit him again.

All too soon, it was dinnertime. Jeff forced himself from his chair and descended the stairs. He was not hungry in the least, but family was here, and they needed to eat.

When he walked into the kitchen, John's wife, Ceci, and Joanne's husband, Josh, were already busy at the stove. The kitchen smelled wonderful, and they had already set the table. Pots were bubbling on the stove, and the two spouses certainly looked as if they knew what they were doing.

They shooed Jeff away.

"Dinner will be ready in a bit," Josh said. "Go and have a glass of wine with John and Joanne. They are outside in the garden."

Jeff walked out to the place he and Dell had lovingly nurtured. While the garden brought him as close to Dell as he could get, he felt as removed from her as he had ever been. Seeing his—*their*—children sitting in the garden brought tears to his eyes again.

Joanne spied him first, walked over to him, and took his hand.

"Come sit with us, Daddy. Dinner will be ready in a little bit."

Jeff sat down as instructed, but he had no idea what to say. In such moments before, Dell had always launched into a funny story or told them everything about a new book she was reading.

John interrupted Jeff's thoughts by speaking first.

"Dad, if it's all right with you, Joanne and I would like to stay here for a few more days. Our better halves, who are so sweet as to cook us dinner, will go home. But Joanne and I can stay at least until the end of the week."

Jeff was surprised by his reaction. He looked at them both and said, "If you are sure you can spare the time, I would love that very much." And he surprised himself at how strongly he felt what he had just said.

Chapter Eleven

MONTHS LATER, TIM AND SHARON HAD SETTLED INTO an awkward routine. Tim spent most weekend mornings reading *The New York Times*, *The Wall Street Journal*, and the *Financial Times*. It gave his mind some consistency, which he craved, and he loved being informed. He was quite aware that he and Sharon had not really spoken more about the elephant in the room. He knew it needed to happen but still felt exposed and vulnerable. His deepest fear was there would never be any change in their present relationship, and they would remain separated, if only in spirit. Tim was not even sure you could call what they had between them a relationship.

Around noon, Sharon ventured outside to ask him if he would like some lunch and if they could talk. Tim was hesitant, but he knew he would have to face conversations with her at some point. Sharon soon had a delicious lunch set on the patio with all his favorite items: cheese, pâté, chicken salad, and good French bread. She even had a bottle of his favorite Chablis.

When Sharon finally sat down, Tim noticed she was sitting

farther away again. He suspected it was because she felt that being physically close while discussing what had happened would be too much for him to bear, and he immediately was resentful.

Tim wanted no sympathy, especially from Sharon. His anger overtook him, and she could tell instantly, so she poured him a glass of wine—a mundane gesture that seemed to relax him.

"What do you want to talk about?" he asked.

"Us," she said.

"Is there an 'us'?" Tim questioned. "Was there ever an 'us'?"

"Of course," Sharon replied, swallowing. She had everything to lose. She looked at Tim steadily, desperately wanting to make some progress between them. To hide her nervousness, she served pieces of pâté and cheese onto his plate.

"I need you to know how much I love you. I know it is hard for you to believe that right now, but it's the truth."

Tim moved uncomfortably in his chair, clearly agitated. He was not sure he wanted to hear any more of this conversation.

Handing him a plate filled with his favorite lunch, she gave him a soft and tender look, pleading with him to listen to her.

"I think we need to talk about this. What happened was just my feeling sorry for myself and wanting more in my life. Instead of talking to you and letting you know that, I took the easy way out and found myself some cheap entertainment."

Sharon's voice began to shake, and it became more difficult for her to speak, but she was afraid that if she didn't, they would be doomed to live as strangers.

"I was afraid that if I told you how I was feeling, you would resent me and suspect me of wanting someone else." Looking down at her lap, she saw that she had twisted her napkin into something unrecognizable, but she had to continue.

"Instead, I just found someone else to fill a void and felt, very selfishly, that if you did not know, there was no harm done."

Looking down at her lap, she said, "I know how wrong that was."

Tim had no idea what to say. What an enormously selfish, egotistical thing to do. He could not understand anything she was saying and could never imagine himself doing something so horrible to anyone else, especially not to someone he claimed to love.

Tim pushed his chair farther away from her.

"Did you ever ask yourself what would happen if I found out? Did you think only of yourself? Did you ever give any thought to how hurtful it would be and what it would do to our relationship?"

Hearing the rage and pain in his voice, Sharon answered defensively. "I felt guilty so often. It kept me awake at night, and every time I thought about it, I got a terrible headache. But I—I don't know. I kept dismissing it as long as I could get away with it. I don't think I understood how my loneliness was propelling me forward."

Tim had not touched any of the food Sharon had given to him. It sat in front of him as a hurtful reminder of what used to be an enjoyable weekend treat.

"Now what?" asked Tim. "You really can't expect me to say never mind and just go forward like nothing ever happened. We will never, ever be normal again. What is the point of being together if it is going to be like that?"

With hands clasped to the point of becoming white, she said, "Please don't say that. Let me try to fix this. I love you so much. Let me turn this around, since I am the one who did all the damage. I know where I made mistakes. I have been seeing a therapist to make sure I get this right. Will you please give me the chance to do that?"

Tim sat quietly, thinking things through. He couldn't see how it would ever be possible for them to get past this tragedy, but he knew he had spent the last twenty-four years of his life with Sharon. They'd married young and grown up together. The thought of walking away from her and moving on alone was terrifying. How in the world would he have the strength to get through his day, knowing he would never see her again? What if he never replaced her?

Tim's face was a picture of pain and confusion. He still had not looked Sharon in the eye, consumed by all the thoughts running through his mind. He started to reach for his food, stopped, and instead picked up his glass of wine. Without taking a sip, he put it back down and let the thoughts roam through his head. Did he want to be one of those guys who was just sadly single for the rest of his life? Was not wanting to be single for the rest of his life a good reason to stay?

While Tim was mulling it over, Sharon suddenly spoke.

"You're thinking this through, which is good, but I need to know what you are thinking. It is not fair of you to expect me to read your mind or try to guess what you are thinking. You can no longer shut me out of parts of your life. We are either in this together or not."

Tim looked at Sharon with dark eyes, feeling his raw emotions overtake him.

"How dare you! You don't have the right to tell me what is fair. You're the one who did the unthinkable."

Looking at a table full of food, he said, "I'm so angry with you. Your betrayal has caused more pain than you will ever understand. It is not easy to say this, but I'm trying, and you should be able to see that. This is not a decision to stay on my part. It's more a decision not to go—for now."

"You're right. You're right," Sharon responded. She covered her face with her hands, as if to ward off his anger. "I understand your anger, and I accept it as entirely my fault."

With a trembling voice, she had one more thing she had to say. "I will do everything I can to make you want to stay and for you to know and trust how much I love you."

Tim just stood up and marched away from the table. Sharon watched him leave with tears in her eyes.

Chapter Twelve

SEVERAL MONTHS HAD PASSED, AND MICHELE HAD FOUND a wonderful nanny who Sam adored so she could continue working part time.

Each morning when she left the house, Michele waved and hollered, "Goodbye, Sir Sam! I will see you later. Then you can show me all the things you were able to do today."

Sam grinned and yelled goodbye back. He was glad to be home and looked forward to the day when he could wave to his mother.

Michele drove to her job, using the time by herself to think about more ways she could help Sam.

"I need to research more to find something that can help me do a better job."

That night, after tucking Sam safely into his bed, she pored over the research chronicling the trials and tribulations of Christopher Reeve, the actor who had suffered a spinal injury in a horse-jumping accident. The story haunted her. How tragic that such a beautiful animal could shatter a life.

As Michele pondered Christopher Reeve's story, she changed the focus of her research. She remembered an article about horses aiding in physical therapy. The more Michele read, the more excited she became. Looking out the window to the back of the house, she thought about the possibilities. After all, she and Sam already lived on a farm and could easily accommodate a horse. Could this be the answer? Could a horse bring some joy back into Sam's childhood? If his two legs could not work, perhaps he could use four.

Michele took a break from the computer and walked over to Sam's bed. Gently tucking him in and brushing his hair with her hand, she glanced out the window. With the full moon, she could clearly see the entire back of the house and the barn. She realized it might become an integral part of their lives. It looked to be in pretty good shape, and she became excited to think they could use it for Sam's sake. After straightening his covers one more time, she returned to her computer with a renewed sense of urgency.

As Michele researched, she found volumes on the use of horses in many different types of therapy. The earliest recorded use was the ancient Greeks.

By 1875, French neurologist Charles Chassaignac had recognized the benefits of horses for therapy.

Sitting back from the computer, Michele looked over at Sam's wheelchair in the corner, then back to the screen filled with people on horseback. She smiled. The horse pictures looked like a lot more fun.

Michele knew very little about horses but had read of people taking lessons. She also noted that the United States required certification for all trainers, hopefully meaning a therapy program would be safe. She bounced between different websites. Some showed pictures of children and adults riding in large, open rings. All had big smiles on their faces. Some pictures showed people just working on the ground with the horses.

Michele decided a horse could be the answer, but she had a lot to do first. In fact, she had so many questions that she really needed an expert. After a simple Google search, she found two therapeutic riding facilities not far from home where she could find just such experts.

Looking up from the screen, she saw that it was already one o'clock. Rubbing her eyes, she felt exhausted and exhilarated. After closing down the computer, she climbed the stairs and crawled into bed, too tired to brush her teeth or wash her face. Still, sleep eluded her for at least an hour while pictures of horses ran through her head.

She quickly took some time off from work and made appointments with the instructors at the two facilities.

When Michele arrived at the first facility, she was early enough to see a class just finishing. A sweet young girl with Down syndrome was taking a lesson, and her smile was radiant. In fact, the little girl was not just plodding around in circles; Brenda was really teaching her to ride. The instructor had the horse on a long line and asked the young girl to raise her arms over her head and then bring them down and out to the sides. This would help her balance on the horse's back. The instructor then had her touch her nose and the horse's mane. She had her look to the rear of the horse and then pat the horse on his back behind the saddle. One instruction followed another, and the girl was ecstatic when she finally dismounted with an obvious feeling of accomplishment. Michele sensed that something good might be about to happen.

There were no lessons at the second facility, so Michele had a long conversation with the owner, Alice, who was also the instructor. Brenda was a tall woman with a masculine voice and a blunt way of speaking. She was proud of herself and her skills in dealing with her students. Often, she had to determine whether a student needed a push or needed more time to conquer their fears. She brought Michele a sense of reality, however. Not just any horse was capable of therapeutic riding, and even the easiest horses in the world required a significant amount of work and training. Brenda warned that buying a horse was not like bringing home a puppy.

Michele was very grateful for Brenda's time and information. Making a quick decision, she said to Brenda, "I am ready to move forward with this. Will you help? I need a horse, and I would be thrilled if you would agree to give Sam lessons."

"I would love that," Brenda said. "I don't often travel to teach, but in this case, I would be interested. I spent a good deal of time training for the situation you have described, but I haven't had the opportunity to work with any children who are considered paraplegic." She moved through the barn, doing chores. "But first, let me do some research to see if we can find the perfect horse for Sam."

They continued their conversation as Brenda strode around the facility. It was close to noon, and the horses needed their lunchtime hay and rub on their noses. As they reached the end of the aisle, Brenda walked outside and pointed Michele toward a golf cart. She turned the key and she yelled out in a clear voice, "Come on, kids!"

Michele's eyes popped wide open when she saw two of the cutest goats run out of the shed and jump into the back seat of the cart. As soon as they settled in, Brenda took off to the end of the long driveway. She had a fence that needed repair, and her pygmy goats loved to eat the kudzu on the outside of the pasture.

"Meet Thomas and Cynthia," she said with a laugh, giving

them each a scratch on the head. Brenda, being Brenda, jumped back into their previous conversation.

"In the meantime, I see by your address that you live very close to Jeff Dunn. I know Jeff. He's very knowledgeable about horses. His family was in the horse business for many years. Whenever they sold a new horse to someone, Jeff volunteered to help the new partnership develop. He can help find the right horse for Sam, and he also will be able to tell you if your farm has all you need to provide a good home."

She pulled out her phone and found his contact information.

"I will give you his number. You should call him and see if he will come to your farm and tell you what you will need."

After fixing a loose board with a large amount of duct tape, Brenda climbed back into the golf cart. "I take a very personal approach to having a horse arrive and live with a family. I need to know that they will be well taken care of."

Calling for the goats, she drove back to the barn. Once there, she shook hands with Michele and was about to send her on her way.

"One more thing," Brenda said. "You cannot have a horse living on your property alone. They are herd animals, and whatever animal you and Jeff decide on will need a friend to live in the barn with them. I have the perfect goat for you to adopt to be that friend. Does that work for you?"

Michele looked at Brenda, grinned, and said, "Whatever it takes! I will call Mr. Dunn this afternoon. Thank you again. I truly appreciate all your help, and what a wonderful place you have here."

She went home feeling excited and a little bit nervous, thinking, *What in the world have I gotten myself into?*

Brenda had given Michele enough information that she knew this would not be a small undertaking. She looked out her window toward the barn, wondering if it could possibly work. Then she called Jeff. She was a little nervous to call a complete stranger to ask for help, but she was living in a new world now. She had to look for and accept help.

Once she explained who she was and why she was calling, Jeff immediately agreed to come to her farm and see what they needed to do. He was thrilled to do so.

That night, Michele crawled into her bed, pulled the covers up to her chin, and stared at the ceiling. This would be a new chapter in her life, and she wondered if she was up to the task. She thought more about her conversation with Jeff, rolled over, and threw the extra pillow off the bed. As she closed her eyes, she thought, *Time to ask for help…wherever.*

Chapter Thirteen

AS IS USUAL IN THE COUNTRY, JEFF KNOCKED ON THE back door when he arrived at the farm. Michele and Sam were in the kitchen and invited him in.

"Jeff, I can't thank you enough for helping me out. Oh, and this is Sam."

Jeff nodded to Sam and said to Michele, "I'm so happy that Brenda had you give me a call. I've missed being involved in the horse world. I'm going to have to go over to her facility. How about if we go on out back and have a look at your place to see if it'll need anything?"

The three of them proceeded out to the back of the house to inspect the property. Jeff was pleasantly surprised to see there was a small but very tidy barn surrounded by fencing. It would need some work, but not enough to create an impossible financial burden.

Since he had recently retired, Jeff was ready, willing, and able to do some of the work himself. He relished the challenge and was excited to have a project to keep his mind and hands occupied.

When they reached the front porch with the ramp, he reached for Sam's chair and said, "May I?"

"Of course," Michele responded. "Any help is greatly appreciated."

As Jeff pushed Sam along toward the barn, Michele looked over and told him, "I am embarrassed to say that I have no knowledge of horses at all. But there is something about this that seems right to me. You can't imagine how grateful I am for your help."

Jeff smiled and responded, "I'll be honest with you and tell you that I am excited to work with you and Sam. I spent many years working with horses, and it always gave me complete joy. Working with Sam will be a new venture for me, but I am really looking forward to that as well."

He pushed Sam's chair around to face him and asked, "You ready for an adventure, Sam?"

"You bet!" Sam said.

All three walked through the barn. Jeff pulled open cabinets, shoved open doors, and even climbed a pair of rickety stairs to look at the hayloft.

Two stalls opened into the barn and also to the outside. The lights, miraculously, all worked, and though no water came out from the water pumps, Jeff assumed they had just been turned off for the winter.

As Jeff worked his way through the barn, he informed Michele and Sam what he was looking for and why.

Sam had one big question: "Do you think I can really ride a horse?"

Jeff smiled and nodded his head. "Not to brag, but I can teach anyone to ride. You wait and see."

After he finished his inspection of the barn, Michele called Brenda to report what they had discussed and to advise her that Jeff would inquire about a horse suitable for Sam.

Michele walked to the end of the driveway, pushing Sam in his chair. She waved goodbye and then dropped her hand to Sam's head and rubbed his hair as they watched Jeff drive away.

When Jeff got home, he went straight to the kitchen to grab some lunch. After a quick survey of what he had in his refrigerator, he started pulling one item after another and putting them on the counter. He soon had a large sandwich stuffed with meats, cheeses, and plenty of mustard. He set it all out on a plate next to a tall glass of iced tea. His appetite, which had been sorely lacking, returned simply because he was looking forward to something he loved to do.

He still desperately missed Dell, and the intervening months had not made that any easier. Adjusting to a life without her was not going well. He managed to get up and out of bed in the mornings, but he was so out of sorts, he seemed to get nothing done during the day. He had not even spent much time in his garden. It felt like such a lonely place without his wife digging next to him.

He knew it was time for a change.

Jeff had already learned from Sam. He asked many good questions and seemed eager to start on a new project, despite being in a wheelchair. As Jeff toured the farm, Sam followed him through the entire inspection.

"How big will the horse be?" he asked. "Will it bite? Oh, and Mommy said that we were also going to get a goat! That is so cool. I don't know anybody who has a goat."

Jeff kept his answers simple and told Sam that he would make sure to get the right size horse, and absolutely one that would not bite! Sam even made Jeff laugh a couple of times.

After dinner that evening, Jeff was so excited that he called his children and regaled them with all he had done that day and what he would do in the coming months. Both were amazed to hear of his returning to the horse world. They knew about his past but had never seen him with horses. Yet the sound of his voice comforted them.

In the next days, Jeff compiled a list of the things the farm would need. He also made time to visit Brenda. They knew they could find the right horse for Sam because if the horse had the right temperament, Jeff had the knowledge to train him to be a perfect therapeutic riding horse, and Brenda felt confident she could help Sam learn to ride.

Jeff arrived early at the tractor supply store; the staff were just unlocking the doors. Roaming the aisles, he had to restrain himself from going overboard on purchases for the barn. He pulled down feeding bins, hooks, buckets, shovels, and just about everything he could think of to have the barn in tip-top shape for a new horse.

Jeff knew there would be a lot of training involved, and he relished the idea. He remembered the feeling of first arriving in the barn. The smell of leather, hay, and wood made him stop and recognize how he had enjoyed every day.

By the end of the week, he had a list of six horses to see. He had been very careful about telling the owners what he wanted so he did not spend time looking at horses entirely inappropriate for Sam's needs.

Michele agreed to leave the choice of the animal to Jeff. Not only did Michele have very little knowledge of horses, but despite only knowing Jeff for a short time, she trusted him to put Sam's well-being and safety first. Jeff had called several times to question Michele about where the power lines were and where the water came from. Each time, Michele was impressed by his knowledge. Jeff seemed completely at ease with Sam. Sam had many questions for Jeff, who answered them all in a way that was easy for Sam to understand. At one point in the conversation, Michele wondered whether she even needed to be there. *It must be a guy thing,* she thought.

Jeff's first stop was a charming farmette about five miles away. The horse for sale was a quiet little mare named Indie.

As Jeff walked into the paddock, the mare gave him a quiet stare. He could see the intelligence in her beautiful brown eyes. Soon she walked to him and nudged him with her nose. He took that time to look her over. She stood absolutely still while he poked and prodded her. He checked her teeth and picked up her feet. Scratching Indie behind her ears, he asked the owner many questions about her health and temperament. She was just the right size and age, but more importantly, Jeff knew mares were often very maternal. They were a little more difficult to begin with, but once they knew you, understood you, and trusted you, they were the most caring creatures.

The second farm had a lovely gelding, but Jeff was concerned by his conformation. The gelding was a good-looking quarter horse, but years of inbreeding had created some quarter horses with strong-muscled bodies tottering on very small feet. The last thing he wanted to do was bring Michele and Sam a horse that would be sick and cost them a great deal of money in vet bills.

Farm number three had another mare, and she was a distinct possibility.

By the end of the second day, Jeff had managed to visit all six farms. By far, the first farm with the gentle little mare was his choice. Michele, Sam, and Jeff drove to the farm to complete the sale. Sam's eyes grew so large and so happy at his introduction to Indie that the whole group grinned ear to ear for the entire negotiation.

Jeff took his role of advisor very seriously and handled all the negotiations. He even had the owner agree to a two-week trial period before Michele paid for Indie. The owner agreed, as long as Michele bought insurance on Indie to cover any injuries during the trial period. Things went so well, in fact, that the owner even promised to bring the horse to their farm and help to get her settled in, including bringing food and hay so Indie would immediately feel at home. The negotiations ended before they really began with a quick deal that delighted all.

They left the barn area elated, and Indie settled into step with them and walked quietly next to Sam. She instinctively sensed she had found a new best friend.

By week's end, Jeff had the barn in tip-top shape and had everything in place to allow Indie to settle in on Saturday. Sam, Michele, and Jeff were up at the crack of dawn that day. Each was excited for different reasons.

As they walked into the newly fixed-up barn, Michele offered Jeff a large mug of steaming coffee, and the three of them absorbed all the smells and beauty of their new adventure.

They had picked up Mickie, their new goat, the day before. He was busy checking out the surroundings, and every now and then, he plopped right down in front of Sam's wheelchair as if looking for a treat. This gave Sam a good case of the giggles. Michele was excited thinking about Sam being able to learn something new and having a new friend. Sam was thrilled to have his very own pet, and the thought of riding Indie through the field was intoxicating. Jeff was excited to get back into the world of horses, and he was looking forward to helping Sam learn everything he could about having a pet like Indie.

By ten thirty, Peggy, Indie's owner, called to say she was at the gas station on their road, and she would be to Michele's farm in about twenty minutes.

While Peggy was filling her truck, another woman drove into the station. The woman took one look at the trailer and came over to talk. Sharon peeked through the open slats and looked directly into Indie's eyes. She took in the beautiful horse smell and ached to touch her soft nose. Sharon was beautiful, yet she looked so lost and sad that Peggy felt an immediate attachment to her. She opened the trailer door and asked Sharon if she wanted to say hello to sweet Indie. Sharon reached out to the horse. When she touched Indie's soft nose, she smiled. Sharon asked where Indie was going. Peggy told her that she was going to a farmette on their road for a young boy who had been in a terrible accident. Then Peggy did something that surprised her: She asked Sharon if she would like to come along to the farm and meet Indie's new owners.

Peggy leaned into the trailer to pat Indie's neck. While there, she automatically checked the rope that kept Indie from roaming around the trailer while it was moving. The huge amount of hay tied in front gave Indie something to do during the trip. Sharon watched Peggy and was impressed with her care of the horse, and instead of going about her day, she found herself just hanging around talking to Peggy.

This was only Peggy's second time seeing Michele and Sam, but having spent a good deal of time with them on the day they first met, she was convinced Michele and Sam would really enjoy meeting Sharon. They were neighbors, after all.

Sharon was surprised by the offer and felt a strong desire to accept. The thought of spending her day routinely shopping for groceries seemed boring compared to meeting her neighbors and seeing where this gorgeous creature was going to live. She accepted the invitation with a smile and got into her car to follow Peggy.

At Michele's house, Jeff was waiting outside and motioned for Peggy to drive around back. Sharon left her car in the driveway and followed on foot. She immediately fell in love with the small farm. It had such a warm, sweet feeling about it, and the house and the barn were charming. The house had a picket fence in the front that surrounded two beautiful, tall trees and two Adirondack chairs. Flowers in multiple pots led up the stairs to the front porch, which had still more seating areas. The house had a bright-red front door. It all looked so welcoming.

Michele and Sam came to the back of the house, and Peggy introduced Sharon to everyone. She said she hoped they didn't mind that she brought Sharon along, explaining that Sharon had taken an immediate liking to Indie, and since Peggy knew they were neighbors, she thought it would be all right.

Michele was thrilled to meet another neighbor, and Sam was always happy to meet new people. Jeff shook Sharon's hand and told her she had good taste in horses since Indie really was a unique animal.

Peggy and Jeff guided Indie off the trailer and to her new home. Jeff led Indie all around until he could tell she was no longer apprehensive in her surroundings. He also ensured Indie had a big pile of hay and her stall door was open so she was free to come and go in her fenced area.

For her part, Indie meandered around, sniffing and checking out her new surroundings, and then she decided to approach the fence where Sam was quietly watching her settle in. Indie nickered quietly to him and stuck her nose through the fence for a pat. Sharon, without thinking, picked up Sam's hand and stroked Indie's nose. Both Sam and Sharon were completely taken with Indie.

Sharon was so focused on Indie and Sam that she did not

feel the tugging on her pant leg at first. But she did see something out of the corner of her eye. She jumped when she looked down and saw Mickie.

Sam laughed. "Meet Mickie! He is here to keep Indie company. I now have two pets. Isn't that cool?"

Sharon found herself laughing too. Reaching down, she gave Mickie a scratch on the head.

Indie, Sam, and Sharon all bonded that day.

Sharon was so grateful to be present for such a momentous occasion, and she thanked Peggy, Michele, Sam, and Jeff for her morning at the farm.

Michele looked at Sharon. "You are always welcome here. Clearly both Sam and Indie have taken to you in a very big way. Please come over any time, even if you want to just rub Indie's nose."

Sharon smiled appreciatively. "I'll take you up on that, especially if Sam will keep me company some of the time."

Sharon headed home. As she drove along the country road, the sun kept popping in and out of view because of all the trees. She felt a sense of belonging. She realized she had never felt completely at home in the country. Meeting new people who were so warm and seeing a different type of lifestyle than she was accustomed to changed her perspective.

Sharon's therapist had discussed the need to meet and spend time with new friends. Sharon was not sure if she would be a bother to Michele and Sam, but she felt strongly that she would be able to contribute and that it would be an opportunity for her to heal. Her therapist would be proud of her effort to make new friends.

Jeff drove home full of anticipation. He put down the windows, and air flowed through his pickup. He turned on the music, and one of Dell's favorite songs was playing. This time, hearing the song gave him joy. He smiled and realized he was beginning to heal. Indie was working her magic on him.

He pulled over to the side of the road, thinking of going back and spending the night at the barn. Shaking his head, he laughed at himself, realizing how silly he would look, and he got back on the road. He knew it would only be a matter of hours before he would be back at the barn, feeding and cleaning. With a smile, he began to sing along with the radio.

In the meantime, Michele and Sam moved out to the porch, and with Michele sitting on the hammock, they grinned at each other. What a day it had been!

Sam was so excited he kept looking over at the now-occupied barn and smiling. Michele pushed the hammock back and forth, also staring at the barn. It was impossible for either of them to look anywhere else.

"Sam, how about we have a party? We can invite our new friends. We'll tell everyone it's to welcome the new members of our family. What do you think?"

"That's an awesome idea! Can we do it right away, like maybe this weekend? Did you see Indie come right over to me? It's as if she already knows me and we are best friends. And Mickie is a blast. Can we have the party back here so Indie and Mickie can come?"

"Sure, why not? If the weather works."

Michele was now out of her comfort zone on a regular basis. She had contacted Jeff, bought a horse, and adopted a goat, and now she realized it was time for her to make friends and expand her horizons. If not for herself, then for Sam.

That night, Michele sent out emails inviting everyone to a cookout the following weekend.

Chapter Fourteen

TIM AND SHARON WERE MONTHS INTO THEIR ATTEMPT at reconciliation. They had yet to touch one another and had settled into a relationship of distant closeness and desperation. Tim threw himself into his work and seemed to be away from home more than ever. Sharon had followed through with her commitment to see a therapist but felt that she was not getting anywhere or resolving any problems, especially between her and Tim.

She asked her therapist, "Where are we going with this? All this talk of my past. I want to do something about the now. Can you help me to get Tim to talk to me? How can I get him to love me again if he won't talk to me? I miss him!"

She was aware that they could not resolve everything in a few sessions, but she was anxious to move forward in her relationship with Tim.

The therapist answered, "Until you can understand how you got into this situation, you cannot expect Tim to trust you. You need to focus on yourself so that when it is time to talk, it's the whole and healthy Sharon that Tim is talking to. This healthy Sharon is a whole person on her own, not just a partner to someone."

Sharon understood that she needed to be proactive in the healing process.

She got up from her chair to stretch her legs. While wandering around the office, she continued her conversation with the therapist.

"Okay. I get it, I think. I am aware I need to understand myself better." Sharon also stubbornly stated, "I also know that I am a partner. Tim and I have been together for a long time. We are a couple, or at least we were until I messed up. Jesus, this is hard."

On her way home, Sharon had so much to think about that she managed to give herself a roaring headache.

On Tuesday morning, Sharon received an email from Michele, reiterating how much she wanted Sharon to continue visiting. To make the request more formal, Michele asked Sharon and Tim to a party celebrating Indie's arrival. Michele also intended to invite Brenda, Cathy, and Jeff. She added that if everyone was free the next Saturday at four o'clock, they would have the party at Michele and Sam's house with wine, food, and horse treats.

Sharon immediately texted Tim. *Please, please be available for the party.*

Tim, surprised upon seeing the text, somehow understood how important it was to Sharon, so he texted back, *Of course.*

Saturday afternoon finally arrived, and Tim had chosen two bottles of wine and was ready to go. He had never seen Sharon so excited to visit someone's house before. She wore a pair of jeans and a crisp white shirt. With her hair pulled back in a ponytail and a pair of sneakers on her feet, she almost looked like a teenager. He always thought she was a beautiful woman, but today she seemed as excited as he could ever remember. Watching her, it made him very curious to meet the people who, in a short time, had made such an impression.

Balloons and a sign directed guests to head around to the back of the house. Sharon jumped out of the car with Tim in tow. She was so excited to spend time with her new friends that she grabbed Tim's hand to hurry him along. That first touch felt like a jolt, and it caused them both to stop and stare at one another. Sharon smiled and then tugged Tim along.

Jeff and Cathy were already there, and Sharon introduced Tim to them. Indie, as usual, stood at the fence, wanting to be as close as possible to all her new friends.

Tim was surprised by this new version of his wife of twenty-four years. The way she connected with Sam was amazing. Without a word or a glance to anyone, she grabbed Sam's chair, and the two of them rushed to the fence to visit with Indie. Sharon picked up Sam's hand to rest it on Indie's offered nose, and they seemed to be in a world of their own. Tim was astounded to hear giggles, nickers, and clicking noises coming from the three. He sensed they had their own form of private communication.

Tim finally remembered his manners and conversed with Michele, Cathy, and Jeff. Brenda would be arriving a little late, since Saturdays were full of riding lessons. Michele had to go into the kitchen to organize dinner, so Tim and Jeff had a chance to get to know one another.

Michele set a beautiful outdoor table with plates, wine-glasses, and a wooden cutting board covered with cheese and charcuterie. Jeff and Tim poured themselves glasses of wine and settled into a pair of Adirondack chairs under a gorgeous weeping cherry tree.

"This is just a stunning setting," Tim said. "I have a view of the mountain from my house, but I never even thought to drive farther down the road to see what other homes were like."

"You should see it from my house one of these days. It is at its most beautiful at night around sunset," said Jeff.

Their conversation continued, and they found they both loved country life and enjoyed working on their houses and gardens. Jeff hesitatingly told how he lost the love of his life on the day of the horrible truck accident on the highway. Tim, looking over at Sharon, couldn't help thinking he did as well.

When Brenda finally showed up, she wanted them all to see what she would be doing with Sam and Indie. She slipped a halter onto Indie and jumped on bareback. After putting Sam's helmet on him, Michele picked Sam up and placed him in front of Brenda, and off they went. Brenda wrapped her arms protectively around Sam, and Michele saw absolutely no fear on Sam's face. Nothing but pure joy. No one had ever seen a smile that big on any child's face.

Sam was as close as he could get to feeling his own legs moving him forward. He shouted, "Mommy, Mommy, look at me! I am riding. I am riding Indie!"

Meanwhile, Brenda wrapped Sam's fingers around the lead line, and he used every ounce of strength in his tiny body to hold it. Whenever he lost the line, Brenda just picked it up and put it back into his hands.

After about three times around the paddock, Brenda declared it was enough. Sam was over the moon but also exhausted. What a special moment it was for everyone: Sam's first ride was a huge step forward, and his excitement was contagious.

Michele heated up the grill and dutifully seared delicious-smelling steaks. Jeff tossed his roasted vegetable salad with some white balsamic vinegar and olive oil. Everyone else busied themselves with gathering plates and refilling wineglasses. Each found a chair, and after the first bites of food, the conversation flowed, with laughter interrupting every time Mickie tried to nab some free scraps.

It was one of the best meals any of them could remember.

After finishing his steak and vegetables, Tim sat quietly for a while, content to look at the colors of the setting sun on the mountains. The view and the sound of talking and laughter filled him with a sense of peace. It was a welcome change. He looked over to see Sharon smiling and laughing, and it reminded him of how often he had seen her doing the same even when it was just the two of them sharing a wonderful meal. Filling his wineglass one more time, he joined in again with the conversation flowing around the table.

Sam went to bed while the grown-ups stayed outside well into the night. They continued talking for such a long time that they had to change the candles.

On the drive home, for the first time in a very long while, Tim and Sharon shared a quiet, comfortable silence. Tim was thrilled to have met his neighbors, and despite loving the solitude of where he lived, he realized such good and interesting people lived in the country and were very different from the people he had to deal with at work. He found Jeff and Michele very easy to talk to about everything from politics to gardening to the joy of country living.

By the time Tim and Sharon got home it was quite late, so they went off to their respective bedrooms. But although Tim was tired, he could not sleep. Looking out his window, he saw that the garden and patio where he and Sharon had shared so many meals were highlighted by a full moon. He again thought of how connected he used to feel when he and Sharon shared a bottle of wine and great cheeses and pâté on summer days.

He also thought of how natural and happy Sharon looked at the farm. She, Sam, and Indie seemed like they were already the best of friends.

Wow, he thought. *I've been so blind! Could it have been that lonely for her here? Now what?*

After opening the window so he could smell the night air, he crawled into what was now becoming a very lonely bed and tried to sleep.

The next morning, Sharon set Tim's breakfast up on the patio, and they peacefully read their newspapers. When it was time for lunch, Tim went into the kitchen and brought out all their favorite foods. Sharon was surprised. He had not made the effort to make lunch, as he had in the past, since that disastrous day.

After setting the table and opening the wine, Tim said, "It is time to talk again."

Sharon was ready to talk but a little frightened because Tim had not yet made a serious decision to stay.

He started the conversation by apologizing, which took Sharon completely by surprise. She looked at him with wide eyes.

"I realized last night, while I was watching you with our neighbors and with Sam and Indie, how much fun you were having. It dawned on me that our life here has been very lonely for you. You never said anything, so I really didn't think about it. I never realized it since I was always gone. The time I spend here feels so short for me, but for you it was long days every day."

Sharon looked down, and Tim saw tears quietly roll down her cheeks.

"Why didn't you tell me you were lonely?" he asked her.

Crossing her arms, she answered, "I don't know why I couldn't tell you. I guess I was afraid that you wouldn't understand or would think I was too demanding."

Using her fingers to wipe her eyes, she looked at him. "I know how hard you work, so if I complained about the one place that gave you joy and respite, I would seem very selfish. I wanted you to be happy and to come home to a place you loved."

"Have you spoken to your therapist about this?"

"Yes." She shrugged. "She thought it was something we should discuss, but I didn't know how to bring it up, especially since I am the one who was in the wrong."

He nodded. "You were probably right. I would've dismissed it as an excuse. But after seeing you last night with friends, I guess…I mean, I think I might understand."

Tim moved his plate to the side and refilled both their wineglasses. He pushed his chair out from the table.

"There was something more to your happiness than just spending time with friends. You really glowed when spending time with Sam. I actually don't think I remember seeing you around children very often, if at all. We talked about children when we first married, but then, after a while, we didn't." Pausing for a moment to gather his thoughts, he said, "How did that happen? Was that a mistake?"

Sharon shrugged again. "I didn't think I wanted children. I had no experience with them, and I had my work." It was Sharon's turn to pause to look for what she wanted to say. "Maybe I was just afraid? I just pushed off thinking about it. It is such an amazing responsibility to raise a child, with all the questions that seep into your mind. It is scary!"

Shaking her head, Sharon spoke quietly, almost frightened to make the admission. "I guess I just never had the nerve to give it a try. It's not as if we've spent much time around people with children." Looking down at her half-eaten food, she moved her plate to the side. "We should have talked about it. Now I don't know if that may have been a mistake on our part."

Looking at Tim, she stated matter-of-factly, "It is obviously too late for children now. One thing I do know is that when I spend time with Sam, I feel wonderful." She smiled somewhat wistfully. "I wish I would have known I would feel that way. Maybe I was too immature before. I just don't know."

Tim nodded. Sharon was right about it being too late.

"So what do you think we should do now?" he asked.

Sharon rose from her chair, walked over to stand next to him, and gently touched his shoulder. She stood closer to him than she had dared to for a long time, hoping he would not shrink away. When he did not, she spoke.

"I think we need to work on maintaining friendships here in the country, but more than anything, I think we need to heal our relationship."

She moved her hand to his face and looked into his eyes. "That would mean that we would have to trust one another. Can you feel that way about me? Do you think you'll ever be able to love me again? Do you want to love me again?" Keeping her hand on his face, she nervously whispered, "I also think we need to be able to touch one another. The intimacy we shared was an important part of our relationship. I can understand how difficult it may seem to you, but the intimacy between us was real, not some stupid setup like I created with a stranger. I know that if we can make love, we will be able to be *in* love."

Tim stood and put both his hands on her face. He knew she was right and that if he was going to stay, he would have to try to heal their relationship. It could not be done by just one person, and it could not be done by living in separate rooms. He leaned down gently to kiss where her tears had been and then moved to her mouth. She kissed him back. It had been such a long time that that a simple kiss felt like an electric shock.

Tim took Sharon's hand and led her into the house and upstairs, his heart racing. Was this really going to happen? Was he ready for this? Tim could sense that Sharon was as nervous as he was. He could almost hear her heart racing as well.

When they walked into the bedroom, Tim flashed back to seeing her in that bed with another man, but with great effort, he forced himself to dismiss the thoughts. That man was gone, and Tim was here. At first, he held Sharon's hand so hard he almost hurt her. He realized it and softened his grip. He took her hand, kissed it, and then placed it over his heart. She could feel how fast it was beating.

Tim was risking everything to open himself to this kind of intimacy with her, and Sharon knew she would have to help him in every way she could. She reached for his face and kissed him with such emotion and ardor that he felt his body immediately react. She stopped kissing him long enough to reach up and unbutton his shirt, and with each button undone, she kissed his chest. He smelled so good, and touching his skin after such a long time felt wonderful and erotic.

Tim slowly touched Sharon's arms and then moved to her shoulders. Before he could go any further, he had to feel her close to him. He moved his arms around her and pressed her against him in a giant hug, wanting nothing more than to melt into her so they could become one. The distance between them was one of the most difficult consequences Tim had had to deal with since the day of the accident. For both, the feeling of being physically close was exciting, but it was the emotional closeness they had truly missed.

When Sharon was able to come up for air, she unbuttoned her blouse. They quickly removed the bedspread.

Tim looked at her long legs, which he always felt were perfectly shaped. Her stomach was still taut, and her waist was small even after many years of marriage. She was a beautiful woman, and he took a quick moment to appreciate it.

Lying on the bed, Sharon continued kissing Tim's chest. She placed her hands on Tim's back and pulled him closely to her.

Tim reached for Sharon's hair and pulled back her head, kissing her deeply. The intensity of the lovemaking left them both speechless, and they lay wrapped around one another, both afraid to let go. For five or ten minutes, neither of them moved, reveling in the closeness of the moment.

They fell asleep, and when they finally awoke, it was getting dark outside, yet they were still wrapped around one another. Tim rubbed his hand over Sharon's body. Each caught their breath and felt their heart start to race, but this time, the touching was more important than the full act of making love. The quiet stroking was such a close and gentle way to be one with each other.

After another long kiss, Tim looked at Sharon and said very quietly, "I am really, really hungry!"

Sharon laughed and announced, "That is something I am sure I can fix."

They got up from the bed and pulled on some clothes. Tim elected a pair of soft chino shorts, and Sharon slipped on a wispy midi skirt. They both decided to stay barefoot so they could feel the grass between their toes.

Feeling each other's skin remained irresistible. Tim joined Sharon in the kitchen so they could prepare something to eat yet still be in touching distance.

After setting the table and opening the wine, Tim reclined in his favorite chair in the garden. Sharon lit all the candles and sat on Tim's lap.

With her arms wrapped around his neck, she said, "Thank you. That was wonderful, and I love you more than you can ever imagine. I am not sure if you want to hear that just yet, but I will make sure you know that every day for the rest of your life." She kissed his lips one more time. "I only hope you can feel the same way about me, if not now, at least someday."

Chapter Fifteen

JEFF ARRIVED AT MICHELE'S SMALL FARM NOT LONG after sunrise. He gave Indie her morning grain and hay and tossed out some hay for Mickie as well. He energetically cleaned out the stall, filled the water buckets, and groomed Indie. He loved every minute of the work. Indie was the cleanest horse in existence, and her mane and tail had not a single knot. He often brought leftovers from his meals at home for Mickie, who ate anything and everything. He was also very affectionate, and he and Indie had developed a close bond. Often, when Jeff was brushing Indie, Mickie stood under her belly, just hanging out.

Cathy watched Jeff working while she did Sam's physical therapy. One beautiful afternoon, she brought Sam outside and asked Jeff if he thought he might share some of his work with Sam. Jeff was delighted to have the company and thought he could teach them something. Cathy showed Jeff how to let Sam hold the comb, then put Indie's tail up against the comb and pull it through. Sam's face lit up at not only his accomplishment but also that he could take part in caring for his new best friend.

Immediately recognizing that Sam loved feeling like he had a job he could do, Cathy and Jeff started giving Sam more and more chores around the farm. They hung buckets of water on his chair for him to transport to wherever they needed. Cathy and Jeff improvised and soon had Sam involved in the most unusual types of therapy. It was warm outside, and they needed to carry water from one part of the barn to another.

"Give me hay. Give me a bucket of grain. I can carry anything!" Sam said. He did not seem to mind getting a little wet when going over a few bumps; in fact, he thought it was fun. His laughter echoed throughout the barn.

Jeff seemed to understand that they needed to push Sam just a little to try to get his fingers, hands, and arms moving. It soon became a game between the three of them: Who could think up a new chore first?

In the evenings, when Michele got home, Sam greeted her with in-depth stories of all the chores he had done that day. He bent Michele's ear while she cooked their dinner.

"I groomed Indie today. And I even got to hold the rake against my chair and clean up horse poop," he told her with a laugh. Michele found herself laughing along with Sam.

While they talked, she glanced over, convinced she could see some improvement in his abilities. She was so grateful to Jeff and Cathy for all the joy they were bringing to Sam's life and for making her dream of seeing him work around the farm come true.

Sharon called one Friday morning after the group dinner. She was hesitant, not wanting to intrude, and thought it would be best to offer her services as a babysitter in case Michele had any errands that she needed to do.

"I have no errands, but I would love your company. Could you possibly come over for lunch?" asked Michele. "I really don't get to enjoy adult conversation very much, and I would love if we could just hang out together."

Sharon was delighted and promised to be over by eleven thirty. She felt her spirits soar after hanging up the phone. She loved everything about Michele's place, including the time she spent with Sam. When she got there, Jeff was also there doing chores. Michele and Sharon chipped right in, although Sam let them know what they needed to do and how he could help.

"What do you think?" Sam said to Sharon. "Doesn't Indie look beautiful? I am having so much fun with her. You should see me ride her when Brenda is here. Sometimes we even trot, which is a little bouncy, but it is so much fun, and it makes me laugh."

Two hours and much laughter later, everything was spotless, and everyone was starving. They all moved over to the table where they'd had dinner a couple of weeks earlier. Sitting under the shade of the trees, Jeff produced some sandwiches from his cooler, and Michele got some cold water with lemon. Then they all sat together and had a delicious lunch.

"Jeff, you are becoming quite the chef. Is there anything you can't do?" asked Sharon.

Jeff smiled and said, "I'm enjoying everything I'm doing now. I just wish Dell could be here with me to enjoy it."

"If Dell could be here, I'd let her ride Indie," said Sam, "but if she can't be here, maybe you could ride Indie and pretend she is up with you like I am with Brenda."

Jeff reached over to rub Sam's head. "You know, I think I will take you up on that idea. Dell would have loved it, so I will pretend that she is there with me. Thank you, Sam."

That night, sitting in his kitchen eating a grilled lamb kebab with crisp vegetables from his garden, he thought more about riding Indie. The idea of getting back to riding was so exciting, he had a hard time getting to sleep. He was surprised that he had not thought of riding Indie himself, but he realized that Indie was important for Sam, and it had to be his choice to share her.

Jeff cheerfully followed through on Sam's offer and started riding Indie every day. He trained her to walk and trot fast or slowly. That would be so helpful when Sam started doing more on Indie.

Jeff's children were religious about calling him every week to make sure he was doing well. One Sunday night when they called, Jeff asked them if they would like to come for a visit. He was sitting in his usual chair in the living room, looking out at his beautiful garden, and it surprised him how important having them come home was to him. He told them about the time he was spending at Michele's house and said he would love if they could come and meet his new friends. John and Joanne were delighted to receive the invitation and soon arranged to travel home with their spouses for a long weekend.

The next night, under a full moon, Jeff cooked himself dinner: steak on the grill, along with some zucchini, and a potato in the oven. While tending the grill, he sipped a cold beer. Contemplating another dinner alone, Jeff was happy that John and Joanne were coming. But the main reason for the invitation was so they could see the new life he had made for himself and how much he was enjoying himself. He could hear the worry in their voices when he spoke to them on the phone, and he knew once they met his new friends, they would be relieved. Despite still missing Dell terribly, his life had improved.

After pulling his steak off the grill, Jeff walked over to the garden and sat in his usual chair, although it made no difference which he sat in. At least from this spot in the garden he could see the mountain and all the colors as they changed throughout the evening. It felt good to be physically tired and to have a few sore muscles.

Each morning with Indie and Sam could not arrive fast enough. Walking into the barn and being welcomed by Indie, Mickie, and Sam was a treat. Sam provided constant chatter and laughter. Jeff could never have imagined his excitement over Sam's small achievements. The little towhead tried so hard with every chore and rarely complained or said it hurt or was too hard. While Jeff had allowed Dell to be this connection to his children, he and Sam had a relationship between the two of them, no intermediary necessary.

It's odd, thought Jeff. *I never felt this comfortable with my children when they were this young. Why was that?*

While shoveling manure and piling up hay bales, Jeff thought further. *Is it because Sam is vulnerable? Or maybe it's because of Indie? I know what I am doing with her, and she makes me feel confident and want to share my knowledge with Sam. Or maybe it's because I am older and more mature, finally.*

Jeff just shook his head, smiled, and kept doing the work he loved.

Cathy and Sam's doctors were cautiously optimistic about his progress. Although he still did not have much feeling in his legs, he was showing some small advances with his arms and hands. Cathy explained to the doctors the unorthodox therapy of using farm chores and how it pushed Sam to try harder to move his hands. The doctors loved the concept and agreed that it was best to continue, while cautioning Cathy to keep a close eye on the type of chores. They felt Sam's love for Indie was a great motivator. The doctors also asked Cathy to keep a chart of the types of chores and how long they lasted. They felt this might be helpful to others.

One afternoon when Sharon visited, she took Sam's hand,

put it on Indie's nose, and stroked it up and down over Indie's nostril and down onto her soft lips. Sam looked at Sharon and said, "Soft! It's very, very soft."

Sharon gave Sam a huge kiss, then gave one to Indie, and pushed Sam into the house. They bumped over ruts in the yard, which gave Sharon a fright, but she wanted Michele to hear what Sam had said.

"Sam said Indie's nose was soft! He could feel her skin!" Sharon exclaimed.

Michele gave Sam a big, wet kiss on the top of his head. "You are my best, sweet boy."

She then turned away so he would not see the tears in her eyes, but Sharon noticed and got Sam's attention so Michele could pull herself together.

When Jeff heard the news, he was elated. Standing together in the back of the barn, he and Michele watched Sam slowly move his arms forward and try to reach Indie's nose. Jeff was so proud of the effort Sam made to care for his pets. He decided it called for a celebration the weekend his family planned to visit. The weather was beginning to change, and fall was in the air. There was no better time to celebrate.

"Hey," he said to Michele, "I think this calls for a party. The weather is perfect, and I would love to have everyone at my place. It would be great for Peggy to hear how much Indie is doing for Sam. The party might go on for a while. Would you let Sam sleep in my library if it got too late for him?"

"That sounds like a lot of fun, Jeff, but it might be tough with Sam," said Michele.

Jeff didn't want to push Michele too hard, so he just nudged her arm and said, "Just look at him. He really is a remarkable guy."

Michele responded, "You're right. I have to stop babying him. Okay, we would love to come. What can I bring?"

"Absolutely nothing, except Sam," said Jeff. "I am planning a major menu, and no one will go home hungry!"

Later that night, sitting at the dining room table, Jeff put his computer skills to the test. He researched menus, table settings, and wine pairings. Then he went through his contact list to see who to invite. It took some time to find Peggy's information, but it was important to him that she be able to join them. Horse people always wanted to hear how the horses they sold were doing.

Before long the inbox was filled with acceptances.

Chapter Sixteen

MICHELE'S LIFE HAD SETTLED INTO A NEW ROUTINE after she changed her work hours so she could be home more. The lawyers she had hired did an outstanding job as her counselors. The makers of the jungle gym had settled out of court and agreed to write her a check to pay for the best doctors and care available.

The greatest change, however, came with making new friends. She and Sharon met up many afternoons, and some mornings as well. They took trips to the store together when Cathy was working with Sam, or sometimes they hung out on her porch, just talking. It was as though they had known each other forever.

Jeff was a dream come true. He did so much around the small farm yet refused to take any compensation. He was there early every morning doing chores, and when Cathy arrived, she and Sam went out to the barn to help him.

Michele placed her laptop on a small desk by Sam's bed. From there she peeked out at Sam taking care of Indie. She also heard the shouting and laughter that accompanied each chore. It was the most beautiful view in the house, with the mountain rising behind the barn. If the weather was good, she opened the windows to hear the birds chirping and the bees buzzing. She loved the smell and the sounds so much.

Sharon started to come by more often.

"Michele, what is the latest from Sam's doctors? They must be thrilled with his progress. I cannot believe how hard he works at getting his hands and arms to move."

Michele looked over at Sharon and answered, "The conversations I've had with his doctors have been difficult. I think they try to be positive, but they're also cautious. I understand their position, but it would be nice to get some idea of what his future will be like. I had always assumed that he would grow up, get married, and have a normal life. I guess that all is still possible, but with some challenges."

Sharon listened quietly and then said, "Well, everyone's life has challenges. I guess it depends on how you handle them. You can't imagine how much respect I have for you. You always seem to know the exact right thing to do for Sam."

Michele smiled. "Ask him what he thinks of my not letting him have a TV in his bedroom."

A few days later, Michele and Sharon were out in the back of the farm. The sun was shining, and the leaves were just beginning to turn their fall colors.

"I know it may be none of my business," said Sharon, "but how are you managing to keep all this going? You must have expenses that are through the roof, what with running a farm, keeping up the house, and caring for Sam. Let me know if there is anything Tim or I could do to help you with all this. If I've overstepped, I'm so sorry, but I feel we are close enough that I can ask. Is that okay?"

"Yeah. It's not only okay, it's really nice. Actually, nobody else has asked me about that. It's scary for me sometimes. I've been thrown into a world I know little about. I got a settlement, but I'm not that familiar with investing. I'm just sort of stumbling along, except for taking care of the farm. That I've always done. But knowing what to do with money? Wow, that is a whole different deal. Having money sitting in the bank is new to me."

Sharon smiled. "Let me talk to Tim. He would love to help you, and he's really good at what he does."

After Sharon talked to Tim, he called Michele and asked if he could come over the next night to ask her some questions.

"Sure," she said. "What kind of questions?"

Tim reassured her, "I just need some basic information about your expenses and how much you spend from the settlement each month. Then I can make a chart that will allow you to cover everything you need while still saving for the future. Does that sound all right with you?"

Tim was doing what he knew best. He spent a good part of the next morning in his office making up a chart for Michele. It was even color coded to make it easier to understand.

During some of the visits to Michele's house, Tim tried to give Michele a little history about himself and, in a subtle way, some of his credentials. She questioned Tim about investments, and he always explained them to her in a way she could understand.

How odd, she thought. *How did I manage before all these wonderful people came into my life?*

Days later, Jeff told Michele that since fall was coming, they would need to get Indie ready for the winter. This would include hiring a tractor to come to the farm to remove the accumulated horse manure. Indie was tiny, but she had managed to produce a record amount of manure in the months she had lived with Michele and Sam.

Michele had noticed this. Jeff and Sam had taken it upon themselves to tutor Michele in Indie's care and grooming. To Michele's surprise, she enjoyed every minute of it. She had never realized what a personality came with such a large creature. Whenever she went to the barn, Indie nickered a hello and came over to greet her. It didn't hurt that Michele often came with a carrot or several apple slices. Michele even found Indie's sweet spot, behind her right ear, that, when rubbed, caused Indie to stretch her neck, stick out her tongue, and make something like a soft groan.

Michele often watched Brenda give Sam his lessons, and each time it gave her a sense of joy and wonder at what this amazing creature could do. Indie brought smiles and laughter to everyone around her.

Jeff called one of his old clients to whom he had sold some farm equipment. That client had all the right equipment to clean up the farm and keep it in great shape.

Monday arrived, and Bob showed up at the farm with a dump truck with his Bobcat loaded inside. He drove around back and got right to work. Each time he filled the truck with manure, he drove it away to empty it and then returned.

It took Bob three trips, and when he was finished, the paddock and surrounding areas were perfectly level and clean. Since it was so close to lunchtime and Sharon and Jeff were there, Michele asked Bob if he would like to stay for lunch. He agreed immediately and settled into Michele's kitchen.

Sharon looked over at Jeff and raised her eyebrows as if to ask if he had planned Bob's invitation. Jeff just quietly smiled. They tried very hard to allow Bob and Michele to consume most of the conversation.

After lunch, Jeff said to Bob, "I think it would be a good idea to take Michele outside and explain what you did to clean up the pasture. Sharon and I will clean up in here."

While Bob and Michele were out back, Sharon teased Jeff. "I never imagined you as a matchmaker," she said, smiling.

Jeff smiled back gently. "I was very lucky to have Dell in my life. Michele needs something more than just raising Sam on her own. I've known Bob for many years, and I've been around when he does his work. Come on. Let's peek out the window and see if they are walking around and talking. It's funny. I've never done any matchmaking before, but Bob and Michele are both such great people. I've seen him in all different situations. He has always shown kindness, and I have never heard a harsh word from him."

Sharon and Jeff wandered over to the front porch to spy on Michele and Bob. Watching them walking toward the barn through the paddock, Sharon and Jeff could see an easy conversation going on between them.

"You know, I've even known him to work for farmers who were short on money. He has a huge heart, and he just did the work knowing it was best for the animals and trusted the farmers to pay when they could. He really is a cool guy," Jeff said. "He's a special man, and I would love if he and Michele connected."

Sharon could not have agreed more. She remembered when she and Tim were connected. In her heart, she hoped desperately Tim would one day love her again as he had before she had made such a mess of things.

Michele was so focused on Bob's advice for keeping the paddock healthy for Indie that she did not notice his eyes staying on her face for far too long. Michele was full of questions and peppered Bob for his advice. When they went into the paddock,

Bob watched as Michele immediately went for Indie's right ear. Before he knew it, he was laughing out loud at Indie's antics. Michele just smiled, enjoying the opportunity to show off her ability to make Indie groan. Bob was impressed.

Bob should have left two hours earlier, but he found it very hard to pull himself away. He knew he needed to go home, and he had absolutely no excuse to return for at least a few months. Bob was an honest and forthright person, so he just said what was on his mind.

"Michele, I really enjoyed meeting you and having lunch in your lovely home. So much, in fact, that I was hoping we could spend some more time together. Your paddock won't have to be done again for months, and I don't want to wait that long to see you again. Would it be all right if I called you and we got together?"

Michele was taken aback at what she heard, but when she looked into his sincere and friendly face, she couldn't help but smile. Walking back to the house through what was now a pristine paddock, Michele tripped on a small rut in the ground. Bob immediately reached out and grasped her hand.

With a long look, Michele answered him. "I think that would be wonderful. I don't get out much because of Sam."

Bob nodded, smiled, and said the invitation was for both her and Sam.

A handsome man with a strong jaw and soft blue eyes, Bob really piqued Michele's interest. It took him two days to find something he, Michele, and Sam could do together. He learned of a jazz group playing at a public park only seven miles from where Michele lived.

Bob called Michele and told her what he had in mind.

"It's a beautiful venue at the base of the mountain. The views are amazing," he told her. "I've not actually tried any of the restaurants there, but I'm sure we can find something all three of us will enjoy. Maybe someplace with french fries for Sam!"

"Wow, that sounds like so much fun. I didn't even know that there was a place near here that had that kind of entertainment. I clearly haven't gotten out very much." She loved the invitation and immediately accepted.

Bob arranged to drive to Michele's house so they could use the van for Sam's wheelchair.

Michele was extremely nervous because it had been years since she had been on a date, and when Jeff came to the house to work with Indie, Michele had a large grin on her face.

"What?" asked Jeff. "What's up?"

"Bob is taking Sam and me out on a date! I can't believe it. Oh my god, what am I thinking? What am I going to wear? I must be crazy!" she said.

Jeff gave her a hug. "That is great. Just great," he said with a huge smile on his face. "You'll have a great time. I'm sure of it. And so will Sam. Just enjoy yourselves. The weather should be nice, and if I know Sam, he'll have a blast."

The next call Michele made was to Sharon, who dropped by that afternoon. They completely destroyed Michele's bedroom, pulling out every piece of clothing for her to try on.

Most of Michele's clothing no longer fit, as she had lost weight since Sam's accident. Michele poured a glass of wine for herself and Sharon, and the games began. Sam finally called upstairs to find out what was going on. Michele put on a fashion show for him, running up and down the stairs to get his opinion of each outfit. Sharon found a pair of leggings and a great sweater in case it got a little chilly.

Sam gave his approval and then said, "Hey, don't forget about me. What am I going to wear on *our* date?"

Michele pulled out a shirt he had not worn since he was in school.

"How about this with a pair of tan slacks?" she asked.

"Okay, cool," Sam said. "I thought you might make me wear a tie!"

Sharon insisted Michele visit the salon the next day for a haircut and manicure while Sharon stayed with Sam. Michele needed nothing else—with long, dark hair and wide-set eyes, she was a true natural beauty.

Wearing an open-necked shirt, a sweater, and a pair of jeans, Bob picked up Michele and Sam. Sam, of course, was all big smiles knowing he was going on an outing.

After parking the van, Bob steered them to a spot that had space for the wheelchair and a perfect view of the stage. While pushing Sam's chair, Bob looked down and gave Michele a big smile. She looked beautiful, and her outfit was perfect for the evening. He loved the way she wore only the smallest amount of makeup.

As Bob put the brakes on Sam's chair, Michele smiled to herself in appreciation for Bob's extra effort to make it a special evening.

The music was wonderful, and afterward they strolled through the park. Once again, Bob had done his homework, and they found an attractive little French bistro with outdoor tables and a serviceable wine list. They all ordered the same thing: steak frites. Sam loved watching all the activity on the sidewalk, and Michele loved being out with what seemed like the rest of the world.

As the evening wore on, Sam dozed off in his chair, and Michele and Bob pushed their chairs away from the table and poured the last of the red wine into their glasses. For a moment, no one spoke a word. They just sat back, looked up at the stars, and let out very contented sighs. After a chuckle, they both said at the same time, "What a wonderful evening."

When Bob returned Michele and Sam home, it was close to ten o'clock.

"I'm sorry if I got you home too late," he said.

"Please don't apologize," she quickly answered. "I had the most glorious time. Thank you so much for all the effort you put in for Sam's benefit."

Bob looked into her eyes and said, "I had a perfect evening. I really hope we can do something else very soon."

He gave Michele a very delicate kiss on the cheek, which Sam witnessed.

Once Bob left, Sam exclaimed, "I like him a lot!"

"Off to bed, young man," Michele said with a huge grin on her face.

Chapter Seventeen

THE NEXT DAY, JEFF AND SHARON DESCENDED ON MICHELE'S house. Both claimed they had other reasons for being there, but each stared at Michele until she recounted the whole story of her date with Bob. After some questions and laughter, they both approved and were not shy about letting Michele know what they thought. For Sharon and Jeff, the next step was very clear. Jeff called Bob and told him that he, Sharon, and Tim were coming to Michele's house the next Friday evening for dinner and a movie. He suggested Bob take advantage of that babysitting opportunity to invite Michele out to spend time alone.

"Jeff, I can't think of anything better than going on a grown-up date with Michele, but it really isn't necessary. I think Sam is the coolest kid, and we had a blast on our last outing."

"I know what you're saying," Jeff replied. "I love spending time with Sam myself, but this is different. You and Michele need a little time to get to know one another, just the two of you. Besides, it'll be fun! I've already spoken with Sharon, and we are all on board. Come on. You'll have a blast."

Bob agreed as long as Michele was okay with the idea.

"Are you all sure this is a good idea?" asked Michele in a three-way call. "I don't even know how to behave on a real date. It's been forever. Do people even go on dates anymore? What if we don't have anything to talk about?"

Jeff and Sharon laughed and urged her to go.

"You will have so much fun," Jeff said. "Just relax and enjoy yourself. You deserve a night off, and we will make sure Sam is cared for. And, of course, we will want to hear all about your date the next day."

Jeff, Sharon, and Tim were the best trio of caretakers Michele could imagine.

Bob threw himself into making plans. Waiting for his dump truck to empty, he worked his phone. He googled nightclubs, restaurants, movies, and finally just the word "entertainment." He decided on a great restaurant that was within walking distance of a nightclub. They would have a nice dinner and then take in a show. He hoped it would be a perfect evening for Michele.

Bob's mom and dad had always set date nights, and the planning that went into them was huge. Bob's dad always kept one aspect of the night a secret from his mom. She always complained because she did not know what to wear. But Bob could tell she adored the time and attention his dad put in to make it a perfect evening. Bob remembered the laughter he heard when they got home. His dad took him along on some of his jobs and relayed all kinds of fatherly wisdom.

Bob made sure he had reservations for the perfect table at the restaurant for his date with Michele. When Michele heard the plans, she could not remember ever having an evening of such grown-up entertainment.

When the evening finally arrived, Michele dressed in her

shortest dress with her highest heels. She did her hair in a simple bun at the nape of her neck to highlight her beautiful cheekbones. She wore a very soft peach lipstick and a pair of earrings she'd borrowed from Sharon that dangled almost to her shoulders. Bob was breathless when he arrived to pick her up. She looked gorgeous, and more importantly, she felt gorgeous. In fact, Bob's eyes told her everything she needed to know: that she was truly beautiful tonight.

Bob and Michele had a wonderful evening together, but they never made it to the nightclub. They were so engrossed in conversation that they just lingered at the dinner table.

Toward the end of dinner, they held hands, with each leaning in toward the other, not so much to hear the conversation but just to be that close. There was a magnetic draw between them. They became engrossed in conversation, sometimes interrupting, sometimes asking questions. Michele found herself alternating between elbows on the table and chin in her hands and hands clasping together under the table wringing out her napkin. She was nervous, fascinated, and having a wonderful time.

Curious, Michele asked, "Bob, what was it like for you growing up in the country? I know I loved it. How about you? It was so much fun going outside on Saturday mornings in the summer in my pajamas and bare feet, running around in the wet grass. Did you do that?"

"Something like that," he said. "Except for me it was difficult to stay outside because I could always smell breakfast, and I was starving! On the weekends my dad cooked bacon, eggs, waffles, everything you can imagine."

"So can you cook, or are you just a consumer?" she asked, smiling.

"Well, I'm a somewhat decent cook, but nothing fancy. Just

the basics. Living alone requires a few skills. I'm pretty good with steaks on the grill."

Nervously, Michele asked, "Have you always been single?"

Smiling, Bob answered, "Yup. You don't get to meet beautiful and sweet women very often when you clean farms and paddocks for a living. The few ladies I have met and dated were just never the right fit for me. They were lovely people, but I never felt a strong connection. After several dates, it was almost always clear to everyone that we were better as friends. My parents were very close, and that is something I wanted for myself."

The way he said this and the way he was looking at her felt like such a compliment.

The conversation continued with stories of their childhood and discussions of what it meant to be dating at this point in their lives. Each topic naturally allowed them to learn more about each other. It was a magical evening for them both.

Michele asked Bob about his family.

"Do you have any relatives in the area? Do you come from a big family?"

"No. I was an only child. My mom had difficulty being pregnant, so after me, the doctor said no more. I lost both of my parents about four years ago. I miss them like crazy, but I think about them just about every day. They both gave me so much, and their wisdom and guidance stays with me, even today. You know, I thought about their date nights when I was trying my best to impress you for our date. I hope it worked!"

Michele smiled. "Tonight has been perfect."

After a while, they noticed that they were the last people in the restaurant. They both laughed, and Bob signaled the waiter for the check. Reluctantly, they realized that it was time to head home. Once there, Michele offered Jeff, Sharon, and Tim a glass of wine to thank them for staying with Sam, but instead they had a hearty chuckle at the offer and almost scrambled out of the house.

Bob was about to thank Michele for a wonderful evening and head home when she stepped very close to him and touched his face.

"I cannot thank you enough for such a special evening. I know my life isn't my own and that evenings like this will be few and far between, but I cannot imagine spending the little free time I have with anyone more wonderful than you. Thank you."

Then Michele reached up and kissed Bob on the lips. Bob was not a man of tremendous experience with women, but he did know that this woman was very special, and he wanted to do everything just right. He then kissed her, stepped back, and asked her if she and Sam would be free on Wednesday night since he didn't think he could wait much longer to see her again.

Michele smiled, nodded, and leaned against the doorjamb while they talked. It was such a comfortable temperature outside, and they felt like teenagers, making plans for the coming Wednesday night.

Michele asked, "Can you come here for dinner on Wednesday? I'd like to test out your skill in putting steaks on the grill! I'll cover everything else. Does that sound good to you?"

Bob grinned and said, "You are on! I accept the challenge. Just give me a time."

They settled on eight o'clock so Sam could stay up with them for a little while.

After Michele closed the door on her evening with Bob and her wonderful set of babysitters, she was still tingling from the kiss good night. She entered Sam's room to give him one last check before calling it a night and instead found herself sitting next to Sam's bed and watching him sleep. While looking out the window at the moonlight shining on the barn, she pulled her hair out of the rubber band holding it and shook it out. She kicked off her shoes, gently raised her legs, and propped them on Sam's bed.

While watching Sam, Michele thought back to the years since he was born. The one thing that stood out in her mind was how much of that time was just about the two of them. For the first time since Sam's birth, Michele was pondering not just all the new friends they had made but someone who might become more than a friend.

It made her stop and think about how, or even if, this new relationship could work. She had so many questions. It was late, but she wished she could call Sharon and ask her what she thought. Sharon and Tim had been married a long time. Michele tried to arrange in her mind the things she would have to consider. This new chapter in her life was not just about her. She needed to answer all her questions with Sam as the priority.

Michele had a feeling that Bob had acquired a strong attachment to Sam in a very short time, but would that hold over the long term?

While watching Sam sleep, she got up to pull the covers up his chin. It was starting to get a little cooler in the evening. She gave him a kiss on his head and then just plopped back down in the chair. She was not quite ready to go to bed or to sleep just yet. She had a lot to think about.

Sam, while improving, had a long way to go, and it was very likely he would never live a normal life. He would always need help, and that meant a commitment for a lifetime. Was Michele ready to include another person, no matter how wonderful, in the private world she and Sam had created? Even before Sam's accident, they did almost everything together. The very act of sitting next to his bed and thinking of all the permutations of her future was another act of closeness with Sam. How would this work if another person entered her life? More importantly, how would Sam view another person entering their world? So far, he seemed to enjoy all the interaction with their new friends. He seemed to be thriving on the attention. Michele wondered whether perhaps the world she had created for Sam and herself was too small and not in Sam's best interest. Here was something new for her to consider.

Michele was on the verge of falling asleep in the chair when she heard Sam's voice.

"Mommy, are you okay?" he asked.

"Of course, darling. I was just enjoying watching you sleep so peacefully."

"Oh, okay," he said. "Mommy?"

"Yes, dear?"

"I really like all our new friends. It's so much fun to have so many people to play with and to help me do all the chores I have around the farm. Oh! And I especially love our Indie. She is the most special of all. Oh, and Mickie, of course. He always makes me laugh. You should see some of the stuff that goat eats!"

Michele just shook her head and smiled.

Chapter Eighteen

JEFF WAS AMAZED HIMSELF BY HIS NEWFOUND ABILITY to organize. He sent emails to all his new friends, including Bob, for a party at the house in two weeks. His children and their spouses would be visiting, and he knew they would all enjoy each other's company.

Jeff channeled his dear, sweet Dell and started to learn how to entertain. It was time, and he knew Dell would not allow him to mess up too badly. Going out to see what was in his garden was first on his list because he wanted as much as possible to be homegrown. He researched all the herbs for recipes. It was astonishing how many he found on the internet.

Scrolling through pages of food advice, Jeff was thrilled to see not only what to do with ingredients but also videos on how to mix, mash, blend, and even char most herbs and vegetables. He then matched the food he planned to serve with the right wines and found a way to use his fresh basil in a signature cocktail to start off the evening.

After testing his cocktail, which was a delightful chore, he decided on vodka, basil, lemon, and a touch of sparkling water. While working on the list, it occurred to him to name his drink. The thought of sparkling water made him think of the bubbling water running down the mountainside.

That's it, he thought. He had just invented the Mountain's Waterfall. He was very proud of himself.

Doing all the chores associated with entertaining was fun. That included deciding which plates and glasses were appropriate. Digging through the cabinets in the dining room, he found plates he did not even remember they had, along with linen napkins and gorgeous napkin rings in the shape of horseshoes. They were perfect. He was getting excited to try this dinner party on his own.

When he was at Michele's with Sam, they chatted by the barn, and Sam suggested menu items. Jeff promised he would make sure hot dogs and lollipops were on the menu.

The night of the party was one of the first cooler evenings of fall. Jeff set the fireplace in the living room, and John and Joanne helped him set up the bar, but he shooed them out of the kitchen, determined to do the cooking on his own. His dining room could not hold a large group of people for a sit-down dinner, but he set the table beautifully as a buffet, with flowers, dishes, and candles.

Jeff's children were astounded by how wonderful everything looked, how fragrant the house smelled, and how organized everything was. Jeff had made sure to read everything he could on entertaining, so he had already finished his appetizers when everyone arrived. He had Cornish hens in the oven and rice on the stove, and he planned to sauté the zucchini, tomatoes, and onions from his garden, while adding his fresh thyme and feta cheese just before serving.

As promised, Jeff had also set up a mattress on the floor of his library so Sam could sleep if the adults decided to stay late. He even loaded the television with a children's movie, should the adult conversation become too boring for Sam. He decided on *Spirit*, about a stallion and a Native American man who tamed him. It was a movie Jeff would watch on his own—the method of training fascinated him.

When everyone arrived, they all introduced themselves and tested Jeff's new cocktails. Jeff had set the bar up in the corner of the living room. After making his first Mountain's Waterfall for Tim, Jeff delegated the bartending duties to him and excused himself for a moment to check on dinner.

"Wow! I never imagined basil could be so wonderful when mixed with vodka!" Tim exclaimed. Normally a scotch man, he was delighted to try something new.

Everyone was excited to meet Jeff's children and their spouses. They spread out in the living room, getting comfortable with drinks in hand and a roaring fire in the fireplace. Michele regaled them with stories of the chores Jeff had created for Sam and how they seemed to be helping him use his arms more.

John responded, "You will never believe the imaginative ways he had to make us do chores when we were growing up. More along the lines of Tom Sawyer getting the fence painted!"

As the evening progressed, the conversations grew robust, and laughter filled the house. Jeff took a moment to step back and see that his home was once again a place for joy.

Tim was surprised to realize how much he was enjoying himself. There was no agenda as there would have been with clients, so he could completely relax and enjoy the company. He also kept a close eye on Sharon. Once again, he noticed how happy she seemed with her new friends. And she had a very close connection with Sam, helping him with his food and drink and making him laugh by telling him funny little stories. Sharon was careful to hold Sam's drink for him and cut some of his food, but she also did not do too much for him. A couple of times she glanced over at Michele to see if she was doing things the right way. Michele smiled and nodded, as if to say, *Great. Perfect. Thank you.*

When Tim saw Michele with Bob, he thought he recognized a little bit of what it was like for him and Sharon when they were first getting to know one another. Bob often looked over at Michele even though they were sitting right next to each other. Sometimes when Michele relayed a story of her farm, she reached out and touched Bob's arm so as to include him in the conversation.

Tim was still trying to get out from under the deep sadness and pain caused by Sharon's cheating, and he wondered what had happened to the feelings he and Sharon had for each other when they first met.

He finally shook his head, realizing this was not the time, nor was it helpful to speculate about Sharon and her former lover. He distracted himself in a discussion with Jeff and mused if perhaps learning to cook would be good for him as well.

Tim was learning to find some recreation in his life. Perhaps cooking would be something he and Sharon could do with one another. Looking at her across the room, he saw, for a moment, the beautiful girl he met and fell in love with so long ago. He swirled the wine in his glass, thinking of all the good times they had shared.

He found himself remembering how much fun he had had with Sharon and how quickly they had fallen in love. Once married, their jobs and life took over. Maybe it was time to get off the treadmill to success and enjoy the fun they used to share.

Shaking his head, Tim got back into his evening with some really wonderful people.

Sharon's therapist had recommended that she find new ways of having fun with Tim, doing things they both enjoyed. He desperately needed something good in his life, but more importantly, something good that he and Sharon could enjoy together.

Tim asked Jeff how he had learned so much about entertaining. It really looked like Jeff had a great time throwing the party.

Jeff laughed and answered, "Believe me. This is all pretty new to me, but you can find anything on the internet. And it's a lot of fun once you get into it, especially trying out recipes for cocktails!"

Michele enjoyed the party immensely. It gave her a chance to mingle and an opportunity to see Bob with a group of people. He seemed a little shy at first, but before long he was immersed in several simultaneous conversations.

Bob was the first to notice Sam's eyes getting heavy. He scooped Sam up, took him into the library, and tucked him into bed, where Sam looked up and asked, "You won't forget to come get me when it is time to go home, will you?"

Bob grinned in response and said, "You'll be the first one out the door, young man."

Michele approached Bob as he emerged from the library. "Thank you. I didn't even notice he was getting tired."

With a broad grin, Bob replied, "I liked being able to put him to bed. He has such a sweet smile."

The party lasted for another hour, after which it took some effort for Jeff to convince everyone the dishes were just for him and they were not allowed to help in the kitchen. Michele went to the library for Sam and bundled him into his wheelchair, which Bob then pushed into the van. After many thanks and some laughs, everyone left for home.

By the time Bob and Michele got to her house and got

Sam into bed, it was nearly twelve thirty in the morning. She told Bob it was too late for him to drive home and asked if he would like to have a glass of wine and spend the night at her house. She asked in such a way that it did not seem she was asking him into her room, just to stay over.

Even though Bob was shy, he knew staying over would be better than driving home at that late hour.

Michele went into her kitchen and returned with two glasses of port, a perfect drink for the cooler weather. Sitting on the couch, she reached over to hold Bob's hands. She marveled at how strong but gentle they were, like when he picked up Sam.

Bob turned Michele's hand up, caressed the palm, and then moved it to his lips for a very soft kiss. He then asked, "Is that all right?"

Michele nodded and caressed his cheek. In short order, they were kissing and holding each other very gently and softly.

Michele knew it was up to her to decide how far things would go. Bob was too much of a gentleman to presume anything, so Michele boldly stood up and took his hand. She led him upstairs to her room, and by looking into his eyes, she knew she had made the right decision.

As intense as his eyes became, Bob never lost his gentle touch.

Chapter Nineteen

SHARON HAD BEEN SEEING A THERAPIST EVERY OTHER week, but she felt she was not getting much benefit from it. Her therapist recommended Sharon find some different outlets in her life. She had followed the recommendation by making new friends, and she was spending as much time as she could at Michele's house and trying to meet her out-of-town friends more often for lunch. All the while, Sharon had become fascinated with the progress Brenda was making with Sam and Indie, so she started studying therapeutic riding and realized it could be helpful to people with any kind of disability.

On a slightly cool morning, Sharon watched Sam and Jeff working in the barn. Soon Brenda came by for a lesson. It was very successful, with Sam holding the reins in his hands and even raising and lowering them a little. Sharon stood in the middle of the paddock, watching them go around in circles. She took that time to question Brenda about what she was doing with Sam.

Brenda took Sam into a light trot, and his face just beamed.

"This movement, this connection, this joy is so important to our program," Brenda said, "but it also builds muscle, helps improve balance, and promotes challenges that in turn engender self-esteem. These benefits are very important to anyone, but especially people who have disabilities, either physical or mental."

Sharon noticed the difference in Sam and his relationship with Indie.

She watched as Sam pushed himself to do whatever Brenda told him to do. He never hesitated once, and if he dropped the reins, he tried his best to pick them up again himself. He had the most determined look on his face, and it made Sharon smile.

Sam's love for Indie encouraged him to push himself in all sorts of ways—not just physically, which was wonderful, but Sam also took chances if it meant doing something for Indie. Once he even balanced himself precariously to get Indie a new batch of hay from the stack in the back of the barn.

Though Sam never knew, Jeff always kept an eye on him, making sure he didn't do anything too dangerous. But Jeff was country bred and knew that a life in the country created challenges. Each one that you mastered was a win.

Brenda told Sharon that her barn was always looking for volunteers and that they would love it if she could donate some time. Sharon started helping at the barn about twice a month, learning how to clean and tack up the horses so they would be ready to go when someone came to ride. She often led the horse and rider around the paddock and even had to run next to the horse so the rider could go into a trot. She loved the interaction and the feeling of helping someone else. Sharon soon found that the horses had an impact on her own self-esteem. They all greeted her each time she came to the barn with nickers of joy.

With going to Michele's house, volunteering, and still doing her cartoon work, Sharon felt much more fulfilled. It was a huge change in her life. Out doing things on her own, helping others, she was becoming a better person, someone she could be proud of. While Sharon had always loved Tim, she had focused too much on their time together instead of looking at her life as a separate person who could take advantage of many opportunities. The more she helped others, the more she learned about herself. Sharon was acquiring self-worth, something to sustain herself as an individual rather than just as part of a couple.

She learned that she *did* exist even if Tim was not around. The work she did at the barn was a new adventure. Learning new skills and applying them to help others was a different approach. She loved being at the barn and meeting new people, but most of all, she loved seeing the smiles and hearing the laughter of the many different people who came to the barn for therapeutic riding. They all needed her help in some way. It restored something she had lost: her pride.

She was not proud of how she had behaved, but now it was time for her to become more engaged in helping others, and that included Tim. She knew he was still suffering terribly from what had happened.

Driving home from the barn, surrounded by the countryside that Tim loved, she thought of how their lives had changed. The occasional talks had improved their relationship, but he still seemed sad.

I don't think it is enough, she thought. *We still have a way to go for us to be truly happy.*

She did not know what to do to make him feel better, but she was going to try. She owed him that, and so much more. He was trying to repair their lives, and she was the one who not only had done the damage but was receiving the benefit of his efforts. Any other man would have been gone by now.

Tim did not need to stay with her and yet he did, trying all the while to find and heal himself again.

After contemplating the situation for a while, Sharon had an idea. Since it was a Saturday, she once again got all Jeff's favorite foods and wine for lunch. She set up in the library, lit the fireplace, and put on soft music in the background. Jeff looked pleased and asked what this was all about. She began the explanation she had mentally rehearsed a dozen times.

"Please sit down. I have something I'm really excited about, so please listen. I know you've been having a hard time and that you're still in pain. I know it's my fault, and I want to fix it and see you happy again. We've both enjoyed making new friends, but that's not all that we need in our lives. We need us to be *us* again—the us we were before I messed everything up. Actually, a better us than before. I have a suggestion, and please keep an open mind, okay?"

She got up, grabbed her iPad, and set it on the table between them.

"I think we should go away together for a little while, just the two of us. A vacation someplace special where we can talk, make love…"

Tim started to speak, but Sharon said, "Wait. Hear me out because I have this all memorized! We can just go away and do whatever we want." She put the iPad on his lap. "Look at some of these places. They're gorgeous! I also want to go somewhere we can just have some fun together. Let's do something that will make you smile."

Tim was surprised by Sharon's suggestion but simultaneously very interested.

"Where do you want to go?" he asked.

Sharon had thought the idea through and told Tim, "How do you feel about going somewhere warm, where we can both just relax for several days? And afterward, how about we end our trip in a city where we can see and do things differently from what our lives are like here in the country? Maybe the southern coast of Spain or Italy for warm weather and then off to Paris for a few nights of city living? What do you think?"

Tim scrolled through the pictures on the iPad. The places she had downloaded looked gorgeous.

But what about work? How much would this cost? Tim looked at Sharon's face and saw right away that this was an opportunity for their future. He finally got it. They needed to enjoy their lives now.

Tim was gratified by how much thought Sharon had invested, and he loved the idea. It took him less than a minute to answer.

"Yes! It sounds perfect. Can I let you make all the arrangements?"

Sharon responded with a huge smile on her face, "Just leave everything to me. I will make sure it is the perfect getaway."

Before the week was out, Sharon had arranged the entire trip. Sitting in the large chair in the library in front of the fireplace, she roamed the internet on her laptop, looking at the activities in each city and the lodging in each of the hotels.

One night around six o'clock, still working her computer, she realized she would have to make some decisions. She walked into the kitchen and poured herself a glass of wine. Looking at the label, she realized that Tim loved French wines. That made her decision. It would be all France.

Sharon booked the trip for ten days because they would lose some time traveling. Since they had taken so few vacations, Sharon decided to splurge and buy business-class tickets so they could arrive in decent shape and enjoy the flight. It would include an intimate dinner with wine, followed by lie-flat seats to ensure a good sleep. Sharon booked them into the Carlton Hotel in Cannes, in the south of France. It would still be warm enough to sunbathe and enjoy all the outdoor cafés. After a week in Cannes, they would spend two nights in Paris at Le Meurice Hotel.

The trip would not be cheap, but it would be spectacular.

Chapter Twenty

JEFF NOTICED THAT SAM WAS GAINING STRENGTH IN HIS hands and arms. He called Brenda to see if they could up the degree of riding Sam was doing. Brenda was cautiously optimistic.

"What do you have in mind?" she asked.

"I want to allow Sam to ride Indie without going double with someone," Jeff explained. "I'll train Indie to go on a lunge line based on my voice commands, and I'll put a strap on her saddle so Sam has something to hold onto. I think it will allow him to learn to balance himself, and I know it will make him very proud of himself and perhaps push himself a little harder to work his muscles. What do you think?"

Brenda was impressed by Jeff's understanding of the many nuances of therapeutic riding and saw some real possibilities in his approach.

"I agree," Brenda said. "It's time to take the next step. In the beginning I want to be there, and I'll walk next to Sam and keep an arm over his leg until he learns how to balance. Something tells me it won't take him much time at all. Good thinking, Jeff."

Jeff was thrilled, and he knew Sam would be as well when he explained it to him. First, Jeff would need to get Michele's consent, but he didn't think that would be a problem. She had been on board with all the projects for Sam.

When the lesson day arrived, Michele came out to watch. She had not told Sam the plans. She wanted him to be surprised, and she felt Jeff and Brenda knew more about what would happen than she did. Better to have them explain it to Sam.

Saturday morning started as usual. Fortunately, the weather was in their favor: a beautiful breeze and bright sunshine.

Once Brenda arrived for Sam's lesson, Jeff told Sam he was going to ride on his own today. Sam just looked at him.

"You're kidding, right?" he said, smiling in disbelief.

"Nope," exclaimed Jeff. "I know you can do it, and I know Indie is ready."

Jeff brought Indie out, and she was all ready to go. Sam was happy to see the strap on the saddle.

His eyes were big, and he was nervous, but he was ready for the challenge. Jeff placed him on Indie's back, and Brenda came alongside and put her arm over his leg. And just like that, with Jeff leading, they all walked off. Brenda told Sam to hold on to the handle, but not too tightly.

"Sam," Brenda explained, "I want you to sit up there without holding on. You will soon find Indie's center, and you will be able to balance yourself on her. Soon after that, we'll work on having you give her directions. You'll be able to tell her to turn left or right, to stop, and even to back up. You will have to use your arms to pull on the reins. That is how she will know which way to go. I am sure you can do it. What do you think?"

Sam didn't answer. He was too busy having a blast.

"This is so cool! Wow! This is awesome. Mom, look at me. Look what I'm doing!"

Michele was so excited for him. She could see him use everything he had to do a good job. She would never be able to explain to Jeff how grateful she was for all he had done for her boy. Seeing him up on Indie and so proud of himself brought tears to her eyes.

Chapter Twenty-One

TIM AND SHARON'S VACATION DATE FINALLY ARRIVED, and they headed to the south of France. When they arrived at the Carlton Hotel and checked into their room, Tim was ecstatic. It faced the water, and the scenery was magnificent. The cars driving by on La Croisette, the boulevard between the hotel and the beach, were something to behold: Ferraris, Aston Martins, McLarens, Bentleys, and any other exotic car you could imagine. The room was large and luxurious, with a huge bathroom with towels that must have been two inches thick.

It was time for a late lunch, so Tim and Sharon decided to stroll along La Croisette to see what they could find. There were many cafés, and they chose one, La Piquette, with a table near La Croisette to watch the automobiles and the many people out strolling.

They ordered and then gazed at each other, entranced. They kept smiling at each other, feeling like kids. The people-watching, the sound of roaring car engines, and the smell of the sea were such thrills.

The surrounding tables generated a cacophony of languages—French, Italian, Spanish, Russian, Arabic, and even a little English. After a delicious lunch with a beautiful rosé wine, they decided to return to the Carlton for a short nap.

Walking back to the room, Sharon reached for Tim's hand. The feeling of the warm air and the scent of the sea filled her senses. She admired the water between the colored umbrellas dotting the beach. One hotel had all blue, another hotel had all red. Each had chairs decked out with towels and small tables with silver buckets filled with ice, water, and the occasional bottle of champagne or wine.

Tim squeezed her hand. "I don't know if I have ever felt this relaxed before. This is absolutely wonderful!"

Before going back to their room, they stopped at the concierge desk to book a table at the hotel restaurant for that evening's dinner. It was their most beautiful outside restaurant, with an impressive reputation for fine dining.

After a short time in their room studying the local magazines, napping, and checking on emails from home, they got ready for a much-anticipated dinner. Sharon dressed in her most sophisticated outfit and wore her hair up in a soft bun. She chose a black, fitted, mid-length skirt with a rather high slit, and she paired it with a cream-colored silk blouse, a colorful Hermes scarf, and a stunning pair of stilettos. She looked very chic—very French.

Dinner was unforgettable. The table outside overlooked La Croisette but also had a beautiful view of the water and some of the most magnificent yachts. It was a fantasy setting.

After dark, the boats lit up with stringed lights like floating Christmas decorations. The hotel had placed their table on an angle so they could sit closer together as opposed to across from one another. It also gave them both a view of the water.

They had a glorious meal, starting with foie gras and then

Dover sole for their entrée, grilled and covered with melted butter, lemon, and capers, paired with a lovely white Burgundy.

After dinner, despite feeling a bit jet-lagged, Tim talked Sharon into a walk along the promenade to enjoy the warm weather and look at all the beautiful people parading up and down the street. He even convinced her to have an after-dinner brandy at one of the sidewalk cafés.

By the time they got back to the room, it was late, and they were still adjusting to the time zone. The excitement had kept them on the go, but now they were both exhausted, and after crawling under a soft duvet on top of crisp sheets, they quickly fell asleep.

The next morning, they ate breakfast outside at the same table as the previous night's dinner. The warm breeze called them to explore.

Over their second espresso, Tim asked Sharon if she remembered the movie *To Catch a Thief.*

"Of course," she said. "Why do you think I looked into this area for our trip?"

"Let's go driving on the Grande Corniche. The weather is gorgeous. It'll be a blast!"

Tim told Sharon to sign the breakfast check while he went to see about renting a car.

Sharon paid the check and then stopped in their room to check her makeup and grab a scarf. When she arrived at the front entrance, she saw many beautiful cars but no Tim.

Raising her hand to shade her eyes from the sun, she searched the area in front of the hotel. Tim waved to her from the end of the driveway. He had a grin on his face that was a mile wide, and for good reason. He was standing in front of a stunning silver convertible Aston Martin DB9 Volante, and the keys were dangling in his hands.

"You did not!" Sharon said.

"Yes, I did, and just wait until you ride in this baby."

With his eyes ablaze, he gallantly opened her door.

"Let's go," Sharon said, gracefully getting into the passenger seat.

The roar of the DB9's engine as they drove off sent chills up their spines, and what a perfect day for a drive it was. Tim drove the twists and turns of the Grande Corniche at his usual high speed, and they both knew this was going to be a day to remember.

Upon their arrival in Monte Carlo, Tim pulled into a private club driveway and tossed the keys to the valet. As they walked away, Sharon asked Tim if he should wait for a claim check.

"Not today," Tim replied. "It's rented."

The club was so private and exclusive that it had no name posted anywhere. Tim had only found it by seeing the collection of cars parked in the lot. Since his car matched the others, the valet just assumed they knew where they were and what they were doing.

The club boasted the most elegant, trendy restaurant on the beach overlooking the Monte Carlo harbor. There was sand under their feet, yet tablecloths and fine china, with waiters in tuxedos. Elegant-looking couples occupied the tables surrounding them. Sharon loved looking at the outfits the women were wearing. She also had to gulp when she saw the size of the rings on the fingers of some of the women. Very large diamonds seemed to be the trend.

After they ordered, they both sat back in their chairs and turned their faces to the sun. It felt so warm, but the sea breeze kept them from getting too hot. It took only moments for their bottle of champagne to arrive while the balance of their lunch consumed the rest of the afternoon.

When they finally finished dining on Mediterranean dorado and scrumptious frites, they sat on the dock, dangling their feet in the sea. Tim reached over and covered Sharon's hand with his own. The view and the cool sea air transformed the closeness between them into something magical.

The drive home was considerably slower, considering the consumption of alcohol with lunch. But the slower speed allowed them to fully enjoy the beautiful scenery on display: water views to one side, and mountains and hillsides on the other.

After dinner that night, at the Carlton, Tim and Sharon made love softly with many words of affection. There was something different about being in such a beautiful place. Afterward, they propped up the pillows and stared out the open doors of the balcony. From the bed they could still see the boats with twinkling lights and the moonlight reflecting on the water. If the view was not enough, someone outside was playing a sax. It was a slice of heaven, as if they had entered another time and place where only their love mattered.

By the end of the vacation in Cannes, Tim and Sharon were tanned, relaxed, and more connected to each other than they had been in a very long time. Tim reached for Sharon's hand constantly. Walking through the lobby, even when they were checking out of the hotel, he either held Sharon's hand or draped his arm over her shoulder. They enjoyed their meals sitting closely together and either talking or just quietly watching the world go by.

On the way to the airport for their flight to Paris, each felt much more optimistic about their future. The flight to Paris was quite short, yet Air France managed to serve a delicious lunch of shrimp salad accompanied by a delightful Chablis, and they arrived in fine form and spirits, ready to enjoy the delights and excitement of the city.

The staff at Le Meurice hotel greeted them with a graciousness only a top Parisian hotel can offer. For the check-in, they sat at a beautiful antique desk. A waiter arrived with a glass of champagne for each while the clerk checked them in and the staff delivered their bags to the room. The clerk then escorted them to the room, checked to see if the thermostat was to their liking, and, after refusing the offered tip, bowed slightly and left them. Their room was large and elegant, and the bathroom was simply palatial.

Sharon looked at Tim and exclaimed, "I could get used to this!"

That evening, Sharon dressed elegantly, and she looked stunning. Her white linen sheath made her tan look golden. She matched the dress with a pair of open-toe black stilettos, and she carried a black pashmina. A simple set of pearl earrings finished the look. Tim wore an open-collared light-blue shirt with white linen pants and a double-breasted blue blazer, along with an incredible tan he had acquired in Cannes.

When they walked into the bar, people noticed. Both were anticipating an unforgettable dinner in the hotel dining room, an Alain Ducasse restaurant and one of the best in the city. But first, they slipped into the beautiful and cozy wood-paneled bar off the lobby where fashionable guests surrounded them. After ordering a chardonnay for Sharon and a Glenmorangie scotch for Tim, they settled in to enjoy a small jazz trio.

The music was quiet enough not to interfere with their conversation. Tim was excited to be in the city and wanted to talk about the plans for the next day. Each had a slightly different agenda, but both wanted to spend as much time together as they could.

After about forty-five minutes, they went into the beautiful and most opulent dining room they had ever seen. The staff was excellent, even to the point of bringing a small bench to hold Sharon's purse so she did not have to place it on the floor.

The appetizer of crab cakes placed over a small bed of arugula accompanied a glass of Chablis. Tim ordered the lamb chops and urged Sharon to order the veal for the main course. That way they would get to taste two entrées. Tim also requested a Château Margaux, a 2007 vintage recommended by the sommelier.

Tim and Sharon sat closely together and talked of when they first started dating. Meeting at a college dance was not the most exotic story, but it was love at first sight. After their first date, they both knew how special it was.

They also laughed, remembering their first several dates. Tim had no money as a student, and he still managed to find the most fun things to do. Sharon reminded him of going swimming in the school fountains.

After several glasses of wine, they reminded the other of how fortunate they were that they had found each other. Tim was slightly less forthcoming during that conversation, but they had both come a long way since the morning of the accident. Sharon heard it in Tim's voice and saw it in his actions. She reached for his hand, and it felt wonderful.

As they fell into bed, its softness engulfed them, and duvets and outrageously plump pillows surrounded them. Despite the incredible bed, Tim tossed and turned. He just could not fall asleep.

Sharon felt him vibrating with excitement, but she knew it was her fault for booking their trip to coincide with the Paris car show. Finally, she turned to him and said, "Quit it! You will be too tired to enjoy the show!"

The venue for the show was the Grand Palais, which was within walking distance of the hotel. Tim was so excited that he could barely finish his breakfast. They walked over in about fifteen minutes, on a morning just beginning to show signs of fall. The air was crisp, and of course the taxi horns were blaring.

After about an hour and a half of trailing behind Tim as he looked at one fine car after another, Sharon decided it was time to beg off. She knew by the look in his eyes that he was going to be there for quite a while. Sharon told him she would meet him in the hotel room later in the afternoon. That would allow her to do a little shopping and provide an opportunity for a short nap.

Tim kissed her warmly and looked into her eyes to thank her for such a wonderful trip. "This has been so good for me and for us," he said. "I feel we are finally moving forward."

Sharon kissed him back with a happy smile on her face.

Chapter Twenty-Two

JEFF HAD ACCEPTED SAM'S SUGGESTION AND STARTED riding Indie regularly. She was such a delightful creature, and Jeff had forgotten how much fun he had had training horses in his youth. Sam enjoyed watching him ride, and Jeff kept up a running commentary, telling him what he was doing and why.

Sam asked many questions, and when it was time for him to ride, he did his best to mimic what he observed Jeff doing. Michele, Brenda, Cathy, and even Jeff noticed an increase in Sam's ability to use his hands and arms. Now when Sam dropped the reins, he picked them up on his own, often taking the time to pat Indie on the neck as he did so. He observed Jeff doing the same thing when he was riding. Jeff felt especially good about this, since he now could take some responsibility for Sam's improvement.

Between his own garden and Michele's farm, and now his work with Indie and Sam, Jeff kept very busy. It had been several months since he lost Dell, and he missed her every day, but his life was taking on a new meaning. It was not a complete life, but he was enjoying all his activities.

One afternoon, when Brenda came to give Sam his lesson, she brought a friend with her to learn about therapeutic riding by watching her give a lesson. Jeff and Sam rode double while she gave instructions from the ground. When Sam and Jeff were both mounted, Indie walked around Brenda in a circle. Brenda gave instructions to Sam, and Jeff helped out, but only if needed. It was important for Sam to do as much as he could on his own.

Sam held the reins, one in each hand. With just a tiny bit of help from Jeff, Sam lifted one rein and then the other about three inches above Indie's neck. Brenda then had Jeff hold the reins as she asked Sam to try to touch his knees on each side. He got pretty close and was tremendously proud of himself. Sam's face lit up with a sense of accomplishment and joy at being on Indie's back. Brenda's friend, Janice, was very impressed, and she quickly understood the point of all the different exercises.

When the lesson was over, they all cleaned up, and Janice had a chance to talk to Jeff. Brenda had told her of his experience with horses, and Janice wanted to pick his brain. She followed Jeff and Sam around the barn as they did their chores.

"I know Brenda told you I was interested in therapeutic riding, but I don't know if she told you why. My mother was in a wheelchair from the time I was ten years old."

Jeff offered his apologies.

"Thank you, but because of that, I'm very interested in—actually, no. I am *determined* to open a facility for therapeutic riding. I saw how much fun Sam is having, but I also know from Brenda that he's made some real progress. She said you are the man to see about making that a reality. Is there any chance you would be able to help me?"

Brenda had left to give other lessons, and Janice had to keep up with Jeff and Sam.

Before answering, Jeff took care of Indie. He took off Indie's saddle and led her over to the wash stall. There, he turned on the water, made sure it was not too cold, and handed the hose to Sam. With a look of dedicated concentration, Sam very carefully sprayed Indie to help cool her off and to get the sweat off her coat.

"Okay, Sam. You're halfway through," Jeff said.

Sam dropped the hose, and Jeff pushed him around to Indie's other side.

"Here is the hose. Don't miss any spots!" he joked. "Oh, and Janice, you might want to move over so you don't get as wet as Indie."

Only then did Jeff return to their conversation while keeping a close eye on Sam. He explained to Janice that running any sort of horse facility was a very expensive undertaking.

Janice smiled and shrugged. "I get that, but it is really important to me, and without going into boring detail, I actually have a rather large amount of money…inheritance, you see."

Jeff could tell that she was determined to move forward with her desire to build a facility.

"Okay," he told her. "I'm happy to help in any way."

Janice was not shy, so she asked right away if he would help her find a piece of suitable land where she could build the barns and a home for herself to live in.

Jeff smiled. "Wow! You really mean business. Yeah, I'd love to work on such a project. I see how much good the therapeutic riding is doing for Sam."

They exchanged phone numbers, and after many thanks, Janice headed home. While driving, she thought about what an exceptional man Jeff was. It was remarkable that without even knowing her, he had not only agreed to help her but had made sure she had his phone number so she could reach him at any time. Brenda had given her some information about Jeff, explaining how much he had done for Sam and Michele and his reputation in the horse community.

Jeff got home a little late that night, but he had had such a wonderful day he did not mind. He got himself a small dinner and got right to work on what Janice would need to realize her dream. Sitting at his dining room table, he refilled his glass of wine and started a list. This took him back to the day he purchased all the supplies for Indie. But now he was looking at buying and starting an entirely new facility. This was going to be a real challenge. The more he worked on the list, the more he enjoyed himself. He was doing something he knew so well. He was impressed with Janice's energy and thoughtfulness and was more than happy to help her.

The next morning, after working with Indie, he drove to a nearby real estate office to see what farms were available in the area. When he walked in, an older man greeted him and happily showed him all the properties listed. Jeff went through them, first by location, then by acreage, and finally by what was available on the property.

He chose four of the listings and pulled out his phone to give Janice a call. Just then, his phone rang, and it was Janice. She was calling to thank him again for his offer to help and to ask if he was still interested after sleeping on it. When he told her where he was, she was elated.

"When can we look at the properties?" she asked.

Jeff asked if she wanted to look at the four farms he had pulled off the list. They arranged to meet the next morning at nine at his house, and the real estate agent planned to meet them at the first farm on the list at nine thirty. Jeff left the office with a very good feeling.

The next morning, Janice showed up at Jeff's right on time. She was brimming with excitement, and it was contagious. Jeff looked closely at Janice and realized that she was a very pretty woman. As they climbed into Jeff's pickup, he noticed she was dressed appropriately to walk around farmland: She had a sturdy pair of boots tucked into a pair of tightly fitted jeans. She'd covered her starched white shirt with a flannel to ward off any chill. She looked like she belonged in the country.

Noticing Janice's outfit surprised him, and Jeff shook his head. He desperately missed Dell, and that would never change, but maybe he would come to accept that he had not died as well.

As they drove to the first farm, Janice had a series of questions.

Jeff smiled. "Slow down. We don't have to do everything at once or decide anything today."

Janice blushed and promised to relax a little bit.

When they arrived at the first property, the agent was there waiting. He had the keys to the house and all the outbuildings. Jeff explained to him and Janice that before looking at any buildings, they would need to drive the boundaries. They could always demolish or redo buildings, but it was another thing to change the topography of the land. Any paddocks would need access to water and shade. While they could do this with hoses and sheds, a buyer would still need to see how far they would have to go for water and electricity.

The real estate agent climbed into Jeff's pickup. Driving around the property, Jeff pointed out different aspects of the land.

"You can build a shed here. The land is slightly elevated, so the water will run away from the building. We will have to build at least two sheds per pasture to allow all the horses to shelter when it is raining or if the sun is particularly strong."

"You know so much. I am embarrassed by how little I know about any of this," muttered Janice. Jeff just grinned.

After a quick look at the buildings on the property, they were off to the next farm. It was quite close to Jeff's home, and the acreage was satisfactory for a horse facility. It even had enough space for an indoor arena for lessons on bad-weather days.

Jeff told Janice about his lessons with Sam. "I have found that the more often Sam rides, the more he advances. If you take two or three days off, you lose a week's worth of advances. It is such a blast to see him move forward. If you are successful in building a facility, I would suggest an indoor arena, if possible. It allows riding in any kind of weather, whether too much sun or rain or even snow."

Janice nodded. "Thanks. I get what you mean, and I want this place to be the best it can be."

This farm had a beautiful view of the same small mountain Jeff could see from his house. The ground was level, and several streams ran through the areas where the paddocks would be. Driving a tractor from paddock to paddock and back to the barn area would be a simple task, even for a beginner.

After they viewed all the outside spaces, the agent took them in to see the barn. It was not in great shape because it had not been in use for quite a few years and the owners saw no need to spend the money to keep it up. After a very thorough inspection, Jeff deemed it not as bad as he had first thought.

The inspection was the same as it was for Michele's when he first went to her place. He opened doors, tried light switches, and climbed a dusty staircase to see if the loft would hold all the hay they would need. He even jumped on the stairs to make sure the wood had not rotted out over time. Janice followed Jeff and the real estate agent around the farm, eagerly listening to Jeff ask questions she would never have thought about. She was taken aback by the beauty of the property, especially how it backed up to the mountain.

Next up was the house. It was on slightly higher land than the rest of the farm, which gave it wonderful views from any window. The living room had a giant stone fireplace and French doors that opened to a stone patio. It was a large enough room but not so big as to make it seem unfriendly.

The dining room followed, and although the decor was dated, it was a good size.

"Whoa!" said Janice as they reached the kitchen. It was large, with another fireplace and windows on every wall except one. Another set of French doors led to the same patio as the living room. Whoever had designed this kitchen liked to cook. They had installed top-end appliances, and the granite countertops had plenty of space. In the middle of the room stood a large Viking stove with three ovens beneath, two large and one small. The spacious pot rack hanging overhead had a light fixture and a fan.

The only thing left to excite Janice was the large pantry with many shelves and racks for food and dishes. Janice wandered through the doors to the patio and then back into the beautiful kitchen. Images floated through her head of all the wonderful dinners and breakfasts she would enjoy in this place.

Upstairs were three bedrooms and two large baths. One additional flight of stairs led to a small room with another bath. Jeff could tell that Janice was very happy with the property. She wandered through the rooms with a huge smile on her face. In the room on the top floor, Janice opened the large window and leaned out to look toward the mountain. The view was stunning.

They viewed the other farms, but each felt that the second one was the best.

After they got back to Jeff's house, they spoke for a short while. He told Janice that it would take him a little bit of time to get an idea how much work the farm would need and the cost of getting the place into shape to run a therapeutic riding facility. Janice thanked him profusely for all his help and asked him to give her a call when he had a good idea of the costs.

"Please do not feel you have to rush. I can be patient."

Jeff just grinned. He could tell she was enthusiastic about starting on her new venture.

It took him a full week to make an accurate estimate of how much money she would need. When he called Janice, she asked if she could take him to dinner and they could review the figures. Jeff readily agreed, and they arranged a date, time, and place. He then made a quick trip to Brenda's barn to show her what he had developed for Janice. He wanted her opinion since she already had many years of experience running the same kind of facility. Brenda was happy to share her expertise. She was a great believer in the programs and thought the more facilities, the better. She gave Jeff a few suggestions but nothing to alter the main plan. He then asked her how much she knew about Janice.

Brenda was not one to stand around chatting, so she had Jeff follow her around the barn while she did odd chores. She described how she had known Janice for many years. Taking Jeff into her indoor arena, she showed him the mounting block rigged with pullies that Janice's dad had devised to help larger people with disabilities get mounted. Brenda, still moving and throwing hay into each stall, told him that Janice was very close with her parents and had lived with them before they passed away. She had never married. Brenda also told Jeff that Janice was not as young as she looked. She was just a few years over fifty but had the energy and passion of someone much younger.

Friday night came slowly for Janice, and she was anxious to get to the restaurant. She wanted to make sure they had a quiet table where they could talk. Janice had picked a perfect place for dinner, not too fancy or too downscale. It became obvious to Jeff that she was quite knowledgeable about food and wine.

The restaurant was a charming combination of rustic elegance, with rough wooden tables and velvet banquets. Janice looked lovely in a silver turtleneck sweater and a pair of black wool pants. She had braided her hair until just the nape of her neck. At that point, it became a long ponytail.

Their dinner started with the conversation revolving around the farm. Jeff explained what she would need to get it into shape. He then told her what it would cost to add an indoor arena and fix up the barn to provide enough space for the horses.

The waiter interrupted their conversation to take their order and to open the wine. They both ordered salads to start and then the venison with red cabbage. This was the restaurant's specialty since the deer were farm-raised close by. The restaurant was bustling, and their table was near a window looking out over a charming patio that was clearly used extensively in the summer.

Getting back to their conversation, Jeff said, "When you add all that to the price of the farm and purchasing the horses, you are talking about a good bit of money." He added, "You will never get rich running a horse facility. Even if you rent out some stalls, you'll never make enough to cover the costs of feed, hay, and vet visits."

Janice smiled knowingly. "Let me worry about all that, but since we are speaking about the expenses, tell me, how many people do you think I will need to run the farm? I know you spent time selling equipment to farmers around here. Do they have many people working on their farms?"

"Most farms need to have a few people helping. It depends

on what kind of farming and whether family can help. Some families have more than one generation that all live and work on the farm together. But it is always possible to hire some additional people if you have the means."

"Thank you, Jeff. Good Lord, I seem to be saying that a lot!" she said, laughing.

By now dinner was almost over, but neither was in a hurry to leave.

Janice ordered a glass of port for each of them and asked Jeff to tell her more about himself.

Jeff accepted the port and offered that he wasn't particularly fascinating. He grew up on a horse farm, was an only child, and loved being with the horses. After he got married and his children came along, he took a job selling farm equipment to cover all the expenses.

Looking down at his drink, Jeff started to talk about Dell. "The very best part of my life was my wife, Dell. She and I were perfect for each other. She was an incredible wife and mother."

As he explained further about their lives, he started to relax and noticed he was leaning on the table with his elbows and talking with his hands. This was the first time he had really spoken to anyone about his life with Dell, and it felt good. As the place emptied out, Jeff looked around and realized it had been some time since he had even been to a restaurant. He was enjoying being out and part of the rest of the world. It felt good to be surrounded by other people having fun.

As she finished her glass of port, Janice told him how fortunate he was to have had such a lovely, long relationship with someone he truly loved. She looked into his kind face and took in his quiet demeanor. *No wonder he is so good with the horses,* she thought.

After paying the check, Janice looked at Jeff. "I think you

know how important this is to me. There is no way I could do this without you." With a big smile, she said, "Let's get this ball rolling!"

Jeff and Janice were surprised by how quickly the evening had passed. They walked to their cars and decided to meet again in a couple of days so Janice could decide whether to make an offer on the farm. While driving home, they both smiled, feeling they had met someone very special.

Chapter Twenty-Three

SHARON ENJOYED THE HUSTLE OF THE PARIS SIDEWALKS as she walked back to the hotel. She knew Tim would relish the cars more without having her following him throughout the show.

Tim lost track of time, immersed as an enthusiast at the car show. He saw gorgeous automobiles, with some just prototypes promising a glance at the future's offerings. When he came upon the Aston Martins, he thought what a wonderful idea it had been to rent one in Cannes. A day he would never forget. As handmade masterpieces, they were truly works of art—able to accelerate from zero to sixty in 3.8 seconds.

Tim noticed how thirsty he had gotten and checked his watch, realizing he had been enjoying the cars for hours. He found a booth selling drinks and small sandwiches and purchased some sparkling water and a ham-and-cheese croissant before heading back to the hotel.

Meanwhile, Sharon was off on a mission of her own. She wanted to bring something home she could see every day to remind her of this special trip with Tim.

After a quick stop in Le Meurice, she found a taxi and asked to be dropped off at Les Deux Magots, a landmark bistro in Saint-Germain-des-Prés, a section of Paris adorned with beautiful antique shops and art galleries, and where Ernest Hemingway had lived while writing *A Movable Feast*. When she entered the bistro, the aroma of butter and garlic overwhelmed her senses. A neighboring table sold her on the steak tartare and a glass of red wine. After finishing the meal off with a double espresso, she was ready to shop for the perfect item to display in their home.

Sharon's first stop was an art gallery showcasing beautiful oil paintings, some of which she loved. She snapped a few photos and took a card from the shop. With a quick *merci*, she exited the shop, and because she felt like exploring, she just started to wander. Every block had at least one or two shops, which took quite a bit of her time. The shop owners were all so kind. Upon entering each shop she said, "Bonjour. English, please?" She asked for permission to take photos of the works she really liked. She wanted to look at the photos back in Maryland to help her envision each item and decide whether it was the special piece for their home. Once she decided, she would email the owner and have the item shipped. After visiting at least ten shops and enjoying works of art, she grew tired and decided to get a cab back to her hotel.

She approached the cab stand at Relais Christine, a charming small hotel. While climbing the stairs to the entrance, she tripped and fell hard on the marble steps. Her knee hit first, and as she reached out to catch herself, she heard a snap and felt a sharp pain in her wrist. The doorman ran to her side. Realizing this was a pretty bad fall, he asked her to sit still while he called for an ambulance and instructed the bellman to bring out some ice.

Sharon's phone was in pieces, but she was so disoriented that she could only focus on the pain in her wrist. Once inside the ambulance, she realized she could not reach Tim, and he would have no idea what had happened, nor would he have any way to contact her.

After a short ride to the hospital, she was taken in for X-rays and given pain medications. The doctor reviewed the films and put a brace on her wrist. Fortunately it was a minor fracture and would heal in about six weeks. Sharon was very impressed with the efficiency and professionalism of the hospital staff. A young intern came in to check on her. He revealed he spoke English and had done his residency at Massachusetts General in Boston. He asked what he could do to help, and she immediately asked if he would place a call to her husband.

Chapter Twenty-Four

WHEN TIM RETURNED TO THE HOTEL, SHARON WASN'T there. He surmised she had gone out on her own to do some shopping. She was very capable of navigating Paris on her own. The bed looked inviting. When he awoke after a two-hour nap, Sharon still had not returned. It was getting a little late, and he was concerned. He decided to call her. The call went directly to voicemail. Somewhat worried, Tim decided to give it a little while and try again. He tried watching the news, and after a half hour, he tried her phone once again. Again, it went directly to voicemail. Now he was becoming more alarmed. It was not like her to be gone this long, certainly not without contacting him. Even on workdays, they exchanged texts or sometimes quick calls to say "How are you?" or "I miss you." The fact that they were in a foreign country, where neither of them spoke the language, added to his worry. Tim's mind went to thoughts of car accidents, muggings, or worse.

Tim's phone rang and startled him. He did not recognize the number, but he answered immediately. The caller introduced himself as Dr. James DuBois at the Hôtel-Dieu Hospital and said he was calling on behalf of Sharon before promptly handing her the phone. When Tim heard her voice, he exhaled a breath he didn't realize he'd been holding. Sharon sounded shaky, and a little out of it but managed to tell him most of what had happened. She said she was okay, but he could tell that was not true. He told her he was leaving immediately to pick her up and bring her back to Le Meurice.

As he sat in the cab, caught in traffic, Tim realized how frightened he had been when he couldn't reach Sharon. Despite what they had been through on that horrible day of the truck accident, his love for her was tremendous, and she meant the world to him. Their relationship was healing. The future was theirs, something he had always wanted.

Tim reached the hospital, and the minute he saw Sharon sitting with her wrist in a brace, he once again exhaled a breath he had been holding. He rushed over to her and reached down to give her a kiss. He saw tears in her eyes and knew his love was reciprocated.

That night Tim and Sharon elected to stay in and order room service. They wrapped themselves up in the hotel's giant terry-cloth robes, and Sharon placed a bag of ice on her wrist. They raided the minibar for cocktails while ordering dinner: American-style cheeseburgers accompanied by a bottle of an excellent Médoc.

By ten o'clock, they were exhausted and ready for some much-needed sleep. The whole night, Tim held Sharon tightly, being mindful of her wrist. They spent the next day walking the streets of Paris, window shopping, and they stopped for a light lunch in yet another bistro. Tim never released Sharon's good hand throughout the day.

Their flight home left Paris the next morning. Perhaps it

was seeing their home again, or perhaps it was the ebbing of the excitement, but their incredible Parisian experience made home feel magical and their renewed love irreplaceable.

Chapter Twenty-Five

MICHELE WAS WALKING ON AIR, AND SHE COULD NOT help but wonder why or how this wonderful man had fallen into her life. The more she thought about it, the more she realized it was due to the new and incredible friends she had made on Mountain View Road. Bob started coming by more and more often, and they texted all the time. Soon he was eating dinner with her almost every night.

Bob, Sam, and Michele settled into something of a family. Jeff came over every morning to feed and water Indie and clean out her stall. He always had time to give Sam a couple of jobs or a ride. By the time the bus came to pick up Sam for school, the barn was spotless.

Michele did not have as much time as she would have liked to visit with Jeff, but he seemed to be in a hurry to leave after all his chores were done, so she did not want to keep him. Besides, she needed to get to work as well.

Thanksgiving was just around the corner, and Bob and Michele decided, after speaking with Sam, that it would be a great idea to invite everyone over for a Thanksgiving feast.

Michele pulled out her laptop, and they began to plan for the holiday. Although the list was not too long, it contained many of their best friends. Sam started a lively discussion about the menu. As a growing boy, he was always hungry. As Michele was typing, Bob looked around the room and realized how comfortable he felt sitting there with them. When he looked out the window, he could see Indie in her pasture, grazing by the light over her stall door. Mickie stood right next to her, chewing on some hay. Bob also saw the reflection of himself, Michele, and Sam in the window, and he felt he belonged here.

Michele sent an email to all, and she received answers that very evening. Everyone accepted, including Jeff's children and their families. It had been such an odd year that it just seemed to work for everyone.

Sharon and Tim usually spent the holiday alone, so this would be a treat for them. For Jeff, it would be his first without Dell. It would be too painful to be alone, and his children could see what he had been doing over the past months and how he was helping Sam improve his mobility.

It was going to be quite a crowd, and Michele was relieved when Bob offered to help. Bob reached for his phone and pulled Sam close so they could both view recipes for the big meal. Sam wanted to start with the desserts, but Bob convinced him to focus on the turkey and ham instead.

When they finally got to the desserts, Sam had a long list, which had them all laughing. Michele cried, "Stop, stop. There is no way we can have that much food!"

It felt so natural to be planning such an event together. They deferred to each other and raised some of the same ideas simultaneously. What fun.

Bob's job did not often involve spending time with other people, so his group of friends was almost nonexistent. He associated mostly with owners of farms who needed his equipment and services. That meant he really was a hired contractor and not much more. Although everyone he worked for was very nice, they were not close like a family. He noticed Michele really glowed when she was with her neighbors, either when all together or when only Jeff or Sharon was over.

Bob began to see the gaping holes in his life. He had only known Michele and Sam for about four months, but he truly thought of them as family.

Sitting at the table with Michele and Sam, planning a real holiday, it struck him. The picture he saw reflected in the window made them look like a family.

Why not be family for real? That thought hit Bob like a meteor, and he knew he must ask Michele to be his wife. He loved her and Sam, and not being with them forever was unimaginable.

Now the only thing he had to do was determine how to approach it so there was no chance Michele would say no. He knew her well enough to know she was sensitive to the responsibilities Sam would bring to a relationship. She did not ask anything from Bob in taking care of Sam, but he enjoyed his interactions with the little boy. Many nights Michele sent the two out to the porch while she made dinner. Bob made Sam a special drink with apple juice and sparkling water and himself a cocktail. The two sat outside and watched as the sky darkened, sharing a few jokes. Before long, they competed for who was the hungriest. They teased each other as to who could tell what dinner was going to be from the smells coming through the door. Sam made Bob feel needed and loved, something that brought great joy into their lives.

He was so excited by his decision that he had to go home

early that night to avoid spilling the beans too soon. Michele was his best friend, so it was nearly impossible to keep a secret from her.

The very next day, he went into town and looked at diamond rings. He made sure the store would accept a return or exchange, since although he knew he loved Michele with all his heart, he did not know much about her taste in jewelry. He looked at ring after ring, trying to find the best he could afford. He asked the salesman as many questions as he could. Since he was a very private person, it was impossible for him to ask anyone except a stranger about his purchase. In his heart, he knew Michele was the perfect partner, and he also knew she would love whatever he bought because he was the one who bought it.

He texted Michele and asked if it would be all right if he came over for dinner on Friday night. He reminded her of his grilling skills and said he would stop and buy everything. All she had to do was be there. Bob very much wanted to ask her to marry him in her home with Sam there. After all, he was marrying the family, not just Michele.

It seemed like an eternity until Friday arrived. Although it was only a couple of days, he was ready. He went to a small gourmet store and bought all Michele's and Sam's favorite foods. He carefully selected a Château Margaux and a bottle of Bollinger champagne.

After a long, hot shower, Michele dried and curled her hair so it would hang over her shoulders. She chose a cashmere sweater and a pair of wool slacks, drop earrings, and a pair of low heels to finish off the outfit.

True to his promise, Bob cooked the steak to just the right degree and threw some corn and asparagus on the grill as well. As Bob cooked, Sam sat on the porch and had everyone laughing with silly stories. While the steaks rested, Bob set up a small table on the porch so they could eat outside. It was an unusually warm day for so late in the year.

The dinner for three was perfect. While Michele put Sam to bed, Bob ran to his truck for the ring and the bottle of champagne that he'd kept in a cooler on ice. When Michele came back into the kitchen, Bob took her hand and asked if they could go upstairs to her bedroom.

Michele looked at him and grinned. "I thought you would never ask!"

When they got to Michele's room, Bob took her over to the large reading chair, sat her down, and knelt before her. She looked at him puzzled, until she saw the box in his hand. Her eyes became huge.

Bob took a big breath and began.

"Michele, I adore you and Sam, and I have never been so happy in my entire life. I can't imagine not being with you forever. I know we have only known one another for a short time, but would you marry me?"

Unlike the stories of old, Michele did not start crying. She just touched Bob's face and asked, "Are you sure?"

Bob looked at her with love in his eyes. "I have thought this through. I would never do anything involving you and Sam without making sure it was what was best for us all. I love you with all my heart, and Sam is the icing on the cake. I feel as if we are a family, and you both make my life complete."

Michele kissed him.

"Yes or no?" begged Bob.

"Yes," she said. "I can't imagine living a life with anyone but you. You make my life feel complete as well."

Then he brought out the bottle of Bollinger. They promptly disrobed and spent the rest of the evening making love and drinking champagne.

The next morning, Bob and Michele got up early. Sam sensed that something was different, but he was just too young to understand the goofy looks and constant touching between Bob and his mom. Sam was anxious for his riding lesson with Jeff and shifted his attention to the day's activities.

Bob and Michele decided that Thanksgiving was the perfect time to announce their engagement. Until then, Michele would only wear her beautiful ring at night when she slept. Before Bob left for work that morning, she asked him one more time if he was sure. This was not just any marriage. Having a child already was not totally unusual, but one with a severe disability was. Bob smiled at her.

"I have not a single doubt in my mind. This is everything I want in life."

Michele kissed him as he left for work and realized that this was what it would soon be like every morning. By about ten o'clock, she received the first of many texts they would share over their lifetime.

I love you madly was all it said, and it kept her floating all day long.

It was getting close to Thanksgiving. Everyone was anxious to see Tim and Sharon and hear about their European trip. Sharon had told them of her mishap and reassured them she was on the mend. All the friends were glad to hear she hadn't suffered any serious injuries, but everyone wanted to know more.

A few days after Bob's proposal, Bob and Michele got busy preparing the house for the big dinner, even though it was several days away. Michele placed a tray with silverware and small plates on Sam's lap and sent him into the dining room. He loved the opportunity to make himself useful and participate in the preparations. They set up the fireplaces and chairs so all attending could easily find places to sit, relax, and converse with friends and family.

Chapter Twenty-Six

MANY LONG MONTHS HAD PASSED SINCE JEFF HAD LOST Dell. Although he missed her, his life was moving forward, to his great surprise. Each morning Jeff arrived at the barn and heard his first nicker of the day. The smells and the soft nose that nudged him were pure joy.

After feeding Indie, he threw himself into cleaning the stall and making sure all the water containers were clean and full. This was a labor of love.

While he worked on his chores, he thought of how his life had changed. Nothing would replace Dell, but she might have enjoyed knowing his new friends. And now Jeff found himself thinking more about Janice. He'd been spending more time planning the farm she was going to start. It was a joy to be able to use his extensive knowledge of horse facilities. He realized he had not asked Janice what she was doing for Thanksgiving, remembering her parents were gone and she was an only child.

After he finished his work, he walked over to the house and knocked on the back door.

When Michele answered, he said, "Listen, I know you don't know her very well, but I was hoping it would be all right with you if I invited Janice to come for Thanksgiving. She lives alone, and I thought she would really enjoy it."

"Of course," Michele replied. "I would love to see her again."

Michele was impressed with how focused Janice was on therapeutic riding programs. Sam was proof of how valuable the programs could be.

When Jeff asked Janice to join him at Michele's house for Thanksgiving, Janice accepted happily. It was a real treat for her to have someplace to go for Thanksgiving. She remembered the lovely farm where she had first met Michele and Sam. Watching Sam's lesson was just another reason for her to move forward with her idea of a therapeutic facility. She would also enjoy spending more time with Jeff.

Jeff arranged to have Janice come to his house so Janice could visit with his children before they headed to the party.

Janice arrived about an hour early so she could spend some time getting to know Jeff's children. She came bearing gifts: wine for the cocktail hour and a beautiful cloth-covered notebook for Jeff. She asked him to jot notes about the plans for the farm. It was something she wanted to keep for the future. After introductions, everyone sat down in the living room and shared a bottle of wine.

Jeff's children were exactly as he had described them. Janice told them how Jeff was making her dream come true. Jeff's children and their spouses just stared at him. They knew what a kind man he was, but this was a new aspect.

Jeff was quiet during Janice's descriptions but was obviously thrilled by his new project. He spoke with such self-assurance about the prospects of the new facility, and his children heard the joy in his voice. Soon it was time to leave for Michele's house.

After finishing their wine, they all moved into the kitchen to put away the glasses and help Jeff assemble his portion of the meal. He had planned to bring dessert and the homemade limoncello that had been sitting for a couple of months. Jeff hadn't tried it but was hoping the long time in the refrigerator had made it into something special.

The cars pulled into Michele's driveway, and the party began. Everyone wanted to talk to Tim and Sharon and make sure they were all right after the accident in Paris. Tim found a chair for Sharon as soon as they arrived. Her wrist was healing, but letting it hang by her side for long periods could be painful. They were happy to be back with such good friends. After being strangers in a city, it felt good to be surrounded by people who cared about them.

The sound of laughter and talking wafted throughout the room, along with the smell of delicious food: ham, turkey, vegetables, potatoes, several pies, and plates of cookies. The kitchen table was covered with dishes, and they had to make room for more.

Tim and Sharon brought a side dish and a thoughtful gift for Sam from Cannes: a Hermès brush for Indie. It was beautiful, but more importantly, it had a strip of soft leather stamped with the famous H across the top that would make it easier for Sam to hold while he was brushing Indie. Sharon picked up Sam's hand, put it through the strap, and tried the brush on his arm. It was perfect, and Sam was delighted.

With a small nudge from his mom, Sam promptly thanked them. Just as promptly, he smiled at his mom and pulled her down to his chair, where he quietly said, "You know you don't always have to remind me! I know to say thank you." This bought him a full tousle of his hair.

When Jeff had time to talk to Tim alone, he asked if Tim

was really all right, knowing that having to retrieve his spouse from a hospital in a strange city must have been stressful.

Tim responded, "I thought I had lost her, Jeff. Now I have some small idea of what you went through. I was terrified. I cannot lose her."

Jeff nodded and rested his hand on Tim's shoulder. "If it were not for you all, I do not know what I would be doing at this point in my life. It is so strange that before, we all lived on this road, yet none of us knew each other. What a change it has brought to my life knowing all of you."

Just then Janice joined them.

"Speaking of which," Jeff said, "I would like to introduce you to Janice. I have been working with her on starting a therapeutic riding facility."

Janice told Tim how excited she was to set up the facility but that without Jeff's help, she would not have known where to begin.

Tim was happy to meet Janice. He noticed right away that she was an attractive woman with a sense of style that was fashionable but very subtle. While he talked with her about the new horse facility, he became even more impressed, not just with her business approach but with her empathy for others. He was so accustomed to his many clients, some of whom were always focused on increasing their net worth. Janice, by contrast, seemed to be interested in spending money to help others. The more they talked, the more respect he gained for her and her vision.

When Tim heard more about the facility, he asked a few questions.

"I hope you don't mind a personal question," he said, "but how do you plan to finance such a large commitment?"

Janice looked a little embarrassed and responded, "I was an only child of a very successful man, so I have funds to use in any fashion I see fit. I don't know if Jeff told you, but my mother was in a wheelchair, so I am overjoyed to help others with disabilities have more rewarding lives."

Tim was impressed but practical as well. It was pure Tim. He loved to relax in the country, but he also loved his work and had a great curiosity about new ventures.

He asked her whether she would mind if, after she was set up and running, he spoke to several of his clients, a few of whom were often trying to find worthwhile charities to fund. He added that if at some point she might be interested, he would be more than happy to donate his time to set up the facility as a charity.

"Oh, wow. I never even thought of that," she said. "It would make sense to do it that way. Is that difficult?"

"Not really," he said. "I have done so many that I have all the paperwork saved on my computer. All I need to do is change the names and details. I really would be happy to help."

Janice thanked him profusely and told him she would definitely think it over.

Jeff's dessert and limoncello were big hits with the group, and everyone had to think about loosening their belts a little.

When it was time to leave, Bob did not allow anyone in the kitchen. It was very clear that he had every intention of doing all the cleanup.

As everyone started to bundle up in their coats, Bob jumped up on a chair and clapped his hands.

"Before you leave tonight, I want you all to know that you are our best friends, and we are so pleased that you chose to spend your Thanksgiving with us. And on that note, since you are such wonderful friends, Michele and I wanted you all to be the first to know that she and Sam have agreed to be my family. We will be married in the very near future."

A huge cheer echoed around the room, and everyone surged forward to express their congratulations to the new family, which of course meant that Sam was smack in the middle of all the hugs and kisses.

Jeff and Janice spoke on the way back to his house, and he told her how very happy he was for Michele and Bob.

"I introduced them, you know!" he said. Janice was impressed by how much Jeff thought of others. He could tell that Michele had pretty much considered herself out of the dating world even before Sam's accident. But Sam was such a sweet boy, and Michele was such a good person. He knew someone would fit into their situation.

Janice looked at Jeff as he was driving them back to his house. *Imagine all that he went through, losing his wife,* she thought, *and still, he was looking to help anyone who asked.*

Driving the dark country roads, with his children in another car following them, Jeff and Janice had time to chat. Jeff asked Janice what it was like growing up with a disabled mother.

Janice took a minute to think about her answer. She said, "In many ways we didn't think of her as disabled, except when we could not do something because it would be too difficult for her. She tried so hard to make everything seem so normal. That must have been a challenge for her, but she never complained, and she always managed to fill the house with love and laughter. My father adored her and treated her with such love and respect, and I think there were times when she might even have forgotten that she was in a wheelchair."

"Can I ask you something personal?" asked Jeff. "Starting and running a horse facility is a very time-consuming and expensive task, not to mention adding the dimension of therapeutic riding. Are you sure you will want to be in this for the long run?"

Once again Janice thought for a moment before answering

his question. "That's a good question," she said. "I know I haven't done this before, and it may turn out to be harder than I thought, but I still want to do it. I really am passionate about helping people heal. I learned so much from my mom. Not to mention that, and this may sound like bragging, I do have a huge amount of money. I would like to do some good with it. If I feel like some of the chores are too great for me, I can hire more help. Does that make sense to you?"

Jeff grinned and said, "I like your honesty!"

They laughed as Jeff pulled into his driveway. After Janice said her goodbyes to Jeff's children, he walked her to her car, and they said their good nights. They planned to meet in a couple of days to further discuss the purchase of the property.

Jeff and Janice met again in the middle of the next week and wrestled over how much she should offer for the property. Jeff told her it was perfect for the facility, but the expenses to get it up and running would be considerable. They would need to build fencing, sheds, and barns with stalls, as well as dig wells, and, of course, buy horses.

Janice nodded and thanked Jeff for all the work he had done for her project. "Jeff, I can see that I am going to continue to need your knowledge of horse farms. Will you consider allowing me to compensate you for all this work?"

Jeff looked at her and smiled. "Well, the way you fell in love with the kitchen in that house, I would definitely expect a few great meals! How does that sound to you?"

Janice smiled and answered, "Of course. I'd like nothing better."

Chapter Twenty-Seven

TIM AND SHARON WERE SETTLING INTO SOME NEW routines. Their trip to France had taught them a great deal about themselves. They both realized it was important they spend more time together, talking and enjoying each other's company. They had taken many pictures while in France, and they enjoyed going through them on their computer while setting up a slideshow. Of course, they had taken many photos of the Aston Tim had rented in Cannes, and many of the car show.

Going through the pictures, they also remembered the fear they had experienced. They moved closer together on the couch and leaned against one another.

Sharon rested her head on Tim's shoulder and told him, "When I saw you walk into the emergency room, I have never experienced such joy and gratefulness to have you in my life."

Tim put his arms around her and held her tightly.

Sharon found herself at Michele's house often. She loved hearing all about the plans Michele was making for her wedding, and she was happy to see how wonderfully Bob had become part of a family.

One beautiful, crisp morning, Sharon showed up unannounced at Michele's house. She marched into the kitchen and gathered Sam and Michele at the table. While they watched with questioning looks, Sharon unpacked a large briefcase filled with colored pencils, paper, markers, and all kinds of drafting rulers.

"I have been inspired by you, Sam, and by the people I have met at Brenda's facility," Sharon said. "I now need you to help me. I have decided to create a new cartoon series, and I want the main character to be in a wheelchair. Do you think you can help?"

Michele and Sam were fascinated by the challenge. Sharon pulled out a large pad and started drawing.

"Sam, give me an idea for my character. Should it be a young boy just like you? Do you want him to have hair the same as yours? I know I want his face to look just like yours when you are laughing, okay? Oh, and give me some ideas as to what kind of trouble he can get into, like maybe doing something silly out in the barn. We can even include Indie in the cartoon. And Mickie too. He seems to be constantly getting into something. You guys, this might be the best series I have done. We will make up a partnership, and I will send it to the papers to get the ball rolling on publishing the cartoons."

Sam gave her some stories about his adventures out in the barn, some of which Michele had no idea about, which caused some raised eyebrows. But she loved hearing the joy in his voice as he talked about his exploits. She knew Jeff was always with him, so he was sure to be safe.

The morning flew by, and by the time they were done, Sharon had at least three full cartoons drawn and ready for a light cleanup before she sent them to the papers.

Afterward, Michele made lunch for the three, and they spent another hour discussing the new cartoon.

As always in life, changes were happening. Sharon saw how Bob had made a huge change in Michele's life. Sharon could tell how happy Michele was to have met someone so perfect. Bob had thrown himself into the role of husband and father, even with the wedding still a few weeks away. He had taken over some of the chores associated with the farm, including taking care of Indie in the mornings and evenings. Jeff still came over most days to ride and train Indie, but he no longer had to arrive first thing in the morning to feed her and check her water.

Sam was doing so well with his therapy, and his arms were becoming stronger and more useful. Sharon loved spending time with him. Afternoons passed so quickly that Sharon was almost always surprised to see it was getting dark outside. Sometimes, if she stayed too long, Tim drove over and told her it was time to come home. He was always joking and usually stayed for a glass of wine.

Sharon loved the feeling of having a best friend. She and Michele spent many weekend afternoons together taking Sam to different venues, much like Michele used to do with Sam before his accident. One day they went to the Air and Space Museum. The next they took a trip to the local petting zoo. Wherever they went, they all had a blast.

Several Sundays after Thanksgiving, Sharon served Tim a wonderful lunch before a roaring fire in the living room. Sharon had all Tim's favorite foods, and she included a lovely Russian River chardonnay.

After they got started, Sharon asked Tim, "Are you happy?"

"Absolutely," said Tim, "and I especially love this wine."

"That is not what I'm talking about," said Sharon. "I mean how you feel about us and if you are happy we are together."

Tim was slow to answer, but he knew it was important for them to talk about what happened and what had come of it.

"I am still frightened by what happened, and it changed me, but I also see you have changed. You seem so much more content, and I'm sorry I didn't see you weren't enjoying your life before." After hesitating for a moment to gather his thoughts, he said, "I feel so much better now, and I know the changes we have made to our lives have made a huge difference in the way we feel about one another." While he was speaking, he reached for his wine and stared into the fire for a moment.

He looked back at Sharon. "So to answer your question, yes, I am happy, and every day we spend together makes me even happier. I will never forget the fear I felt when I thought I had lost you in Paris, or the joy when I finally found you."

Again he hesitated, almost as if he had to confirm to himself how he was feeling.

"We are good together. I think we just need to remember to be together and not to get so wound up in our own work and worlds that we lose each other again." Putting down his glass, he reached for her and said, "Does that sound right to you?"

Sharon, loving the closeness, smiled. "Yes, that sounds perfect to me."

They enjoyed the rest of the lunch and the wine and decided the fire was so gorgeous they would just stay there for a while longer.

"I love you with all my heart," Sharon said as she stroked his hand.

"I love you as well. I never want to lose you." He squeezed her tightly and rubbed her cheek with his. "We must grow old together."

What began on the day of the interstate accident with two hearts broken and torn apart had become two hearts repaired, closer and better than before.

Chapter Twenty-Eight

MICHELE AND BOB WERE PLANNING A SMALL, PRIVATE wedding, and although they wanted to have it at the farm, they knew they probably did not have enough room in the house.

Bob, Michele, and Sam got into the van and headed to the restaurant where they had their first date. Sam was chattering the whole way there, excited to be in on the planning.

"Can we pick out the food today? Are you going to get a big cake? What flavor will it be? Can it be chocolate?" Sam exclaimed.

Bob and Michele just laughed, constantly amused by Sam's interest in food.

The restaurant was large enough to have the ceremony in one small room, with dinner in another. Bob and Michele asked to speak with the owner. Hearing what they wanted to do, he was delighted to close the restaurant for the wedding. He offered the whole place from ten thirty in the morning until five thirty in the afternoon. That would allow them to have an eleven o'clock ceremony and a lovely reception afterward. Sam would be the ring bearer, and Michele had asked Sharon to be her maid of honor. Bob had already gotten Jeff to be the best man.

Bob had essentially moved into Michele's house, and they decided it would become their home. He loved the farm and had gotten very attached to Indie and Mickie, and he would never want to live someplace where they would have to be boarded at another facility. He spent more time with them so Jeff could spend more time helping Janice.

Going into the barn first thing in the morning had become something of a ritual. Bob brought a big mug of coffee and sat with the animals, listening to them munch on their breakfast. It was such a quiet, relaxing way to start his day. The weather was getting cooler, but Indie and Mickie generated just enough heat to keep the barn comfortable. He didn't stay too long, since he knew Michele was cooking a large breakfast for him to enjoy as soon as he got back into the house.

Bob put his small farm up for sale. He had a great deal of expensive equipment and rented a large warehouse in which to store it all. He had such a fine reputation in the community for how hard and thorough he was when he took a job that he was busy every day. He was always sure not to book his weekends so he could be home with his new family.

One day he finished his work, drove into town, and went to a medical supply store, where he purchased the smallest electric wheelchair in the place. It was disguised as a small race car. It would be his gift to Sam for a wedding present. After he loaded it into the back of his pickup, he headed home, excited to see Sam's reaction to the new chair.

As soon as Bob pulled in front of the house, he took the chair from the back and hid it behind his truck so Sam wouldn't see it right away. Running up the ramp and through the back door, he called for Michele and Sam.

"Hey, guys, you have to come see what I got!"

They all went down the ramp, and Sam said, "What? What is it? I don't see anything."

Bob walked around the truck and pushed the chair right up to Sam.

"It's for you!" he pronounced.

"Wow, that is so cool! Can I try it, please? That is so cool. How fast does it go?"

"Uh, Bob?" said Michele.

Bob looked over and saw the worry on her face. Reaching over, he gave her hand a squeeze. "Trust me, okay?"

She looked at him and slowly nodded her head. "Okay."

"Don't worry. It is very safe, and I will work with Sam to make sure he knows how to use it. I picture him walking you down the aisle with this. I promise—and you promise, Sam, that you will be very safe, right?"

"You bet! Can I try it now? Please?"

Michele nodded in agreement with a smile on her face. "If he can ride a horse, I guess he can drive a race car wheelchair."

Sam used his arms to transfer from one chair to the other. Bob put Sam's hand on the switch and showed him how to push forward and sideways.

Sam took off down the driveway and turned around before reaching the road. He was a great driver.

Bob grinned at Michele. "I didn't think I would be giving him driving lessons so soon!"

She leaned over and gave him a long kiss and said, "You watch him! I'll start dinner."

The day of the ceremony arrived. It was sunny. Sam would be the ring bearer and walk Michele down the aisle. He beamed the whole way in his new chair, looking at the faces of the friends attending the ceremony. They looked so happy to be at this special event, and he was proud they had given him such an honor. Michele had bought him a beautiful blue blazer with gold buttons, a pair of gray slacks, a white shirt, and a pale blue tie. He looked like a real gentleman. Jeff and Bob stood with the preacher at the front. Bob had a large smile on his face as he gazed at his beautiful bride and new son.

The room was beautiful, with sunlight pouring through the windows and flowers draped over the chairs. Michele had chosen white flowers with a lot of greenery, including evergreen, since it was getting close to Christmas.

She had elected to not go with the traditional long gown and instead wore a smooth silk dress that stopped just above her knees. A small piece of lace covered the straps over her shoulders. She wore no veil and had her hair in a ponytail with one small flower in the back.

Around her neck she wore a beautiful thin chain with a small blue stone. It was her borrowed and blue, something Jeff had pulled from Dell's drawer and handed to Michele, with a gentle smile on his face, before the ceremony.

The preacher started with a short talk.

"The vows you are taking today are not just stock phrases. They are a commitment and an expression of what you hold in your hearts. Never forget to express to each other what is in your hearts."

Tim gave Sharon a knowing look.

After that, the preacher had Bob and Michele say their vows, looking only at each other for the entire recitation.

After the ceremony, which brought tears to many eyes, the restaurant moved the group into the bar for cocktails while the staff changed up the room to accommodate tables and chairs. Everyone returned as the daylight was beginning to dim, and the room sparkled with the white flowers, greenery, and lit candles. Bob and Michele had a table at the front for just the two of them. It was their day to remember, and Bob spent a great deal of the meal speaking quietly to Michele about how happy and blessed he was that she had allowed him to be part of her family.

Sam sat happily between Sharon and Tim. Bob and Michele had decided to redo the dinner from the first date. Everyone thoroughly enjoyed the steak frites, especially Sam. The wine flowed, and the room filled with conversation.

And they served everyone chocolate cake, per Sam's request.

The day was a huge success.

After the ceremony, when Bob, Michele, and Sam got home, they once again sat in the kitchen. The warmth of the room and the soft light shining outside over the barn made the place feel like a real home and gave Michele a chance to examine all that had happened over the last few months.

After admiring the beautiful ring on her finger, she looked around her kitchen table and marveled at how happy she was. Sam had acknowledged his disability and thrived despite it. She was so proud of him. The changes that had taken over their lives had healed her formerly ruptured heart and filled it with love.

Chapter Twenty-Nine

JEFF WAS THRILLED TO BE IN BOB AND MICHELE'S WED-
ding. He got a real kick from seeing Sam drive his wheelchair
up the aisle with his mother.

Standing next to Bob and watching his and Michele's faces
reminded Tim of his special day so many years ago. Watching
Sam maneuver his chair helped him to see how Indie and
the time he spent with her and Sam had done an enormous
amount of good.

As Michele walked toward the front of the room, Jeff smiled
at Dell's necklace gleaming around her throat. It was such a
simple design, which made it all the more beautiful. It consisted
of a white gold chain with a small teardrop-shaped sapphire
that snuggled in the hollow of Michele's throat. Dell had inher-
ited the necklace from her grandmother, and it had always been
her favorite piece of jewelry. Family was important, and Jeff saw
a new family forming today.

About a week or so after the wedding, Janice told Jeff the
offer she had made on the farm had been accepted. The owners

did not live on the farm full time, so she could take possession at any time. She expedited the transfer of funds to the bank, and the farm was hers. Before Jeff knew it, she moved into the house, got the furniture in place, and set the kitchen up for business. She asked him if he had anyone in mind who could build the barn and put in the paddocks.

Jeff was impressed with Janice's drive, and he met with her several days a week to iron out all the details. Each time he was at her farm, they walked the property. They carried small sticks with different colored flags and planted them like seeds to mark where fences, sheds, and electricity would go. He felt a large part of the barn could be prefabricated so it would not take too long to build. It would include an indoor arena so the weather would not hinder any of the lessons. It would also include an accessible bathroom.

Soon Jeff and Janice found themselves in the midst of construction. Workers spread out over the property, putting up fences, building sheds, and running water lines. The property looked like a real working farm.

In three months' time, they had built the barn and put in the paddocks, and Jeff was traveling the countryside looking for horses for the therapy program. Jeff's wealth of knowledge about the horse world was valuable. He found horses with the proper temperament and trained them.

Soon, Jeff was at Janice's farm every day. He loved it and wondered why he had ever stopped working with horses. He knew it was a very difficult way to make a living, but it was certainly rewarding.

Janice was true to her word and invested enormous funds and time into the farm. She contacted local hospitals and rehabilitation facilities to let them know of the coming program. She also reached out to VA hospitals so veterans could join.

As she traveled to the various hospitals and rehab facilities, she left brochures and spent time talking to the patients. Once some of the veterans heard of the program, several of them called Janice and asked her what they could do to help. She told them to visit the farm, and between her and Jeff, they could find something for them to do.

Before long, a line of trucks formed in the driveway and plenty of helping hands joined them on the farm. The veterans did everything from tying buckets in the stalls for feed and water to planting flowers at the entrance of the farm. Janice made sure there was always plenty of food and cold drinks for all of them. When the veterans decided to take breaks, they laughed and told stories with some pretty rough language. Jeff and Janice reveled in all of it. Jeff was even more impressed with Janice when he saw how much she was doing and how well she dealt with the volunteers.

Once all the horses arrived, everyone took a little time off each day to watch Jeff work with them. He had the gentlest manner and never raised his voice. With a soft voice and gentle hands, he soon had each of the animals responding to him as if they had always known him.

He touched them often, running his hands all over them, picking up their feet, playing with their ears—anything to make them feel safe. He became their herd leader. The days were a little colder and shorter, but Jeff still got a lot of training in.

Each horse had its own personality, so Jeff, Janice, and the volunteers understood each needed to be handled differently. The youngest of the group, Seven, needed his nap in the late mornings. He slept so soundly that you could hear him snoring all the way in the indoor arena. It was hysterical to watch him sleep. Half the time his eyes were open, but he was still snoring away. If anyone tried to wake him, he got halfway up, groaned, and plopped down again. It was worse than getting a teenager out of bed.

Hemera, an older mare, was in charge of the entire place. She put all the younger horses, especially the geldings, in their place. All you had to do was to put a person with Hemera and she would become the most diligent caretaker Jeff had ever seen. He tried slipping off her while she was walking and trotting, and she immediately came to a complete stop. She was a true gem for the program.

Jeff quickly realized that riding the horses was not the only therapeutic treatment and started having the volunteers, some of whom had PTSD, work on the ground with the horses. The gentle nature of the animals gave the veterans such a redemptive touch.

One day, one of the veterans with PTSD was working outdoors in the round pen with Hemera. He was trying to get her to come to him by just calling her name. Jeff and Janice were watching outside the pen. Before long Jeff noticed the veteran was becoming progressively more agitated. Jeff knew what the problem was, but there was nothing he could do—a large helicopter was flying over the property, and the haunting sound caused the veteran to fall to the ground, covering his head and screaming.

Before Jeff could climb the fence, Hemera quickly went over to the man and stepped over him. He was under her belly when she reached down with her soft nose and stroked his head. She just stayed that way, stroking him gently, until the man quit shaking. When the veteran had calmed down, she started to nibble his hair and gently urged him to get up with her nose. When he arose, he put his arms around Hemera's neck and held her. She stood stone still, resting her head against his back as if to hug him, until he released her. Jeff had never seen anything like that happen before, and he and Janice had tears in their eyes. When they looked at each other, they knew how important the work was. Reaching over, Janice placed her hand on Jeff's and mouthed silently to him, *Thank you.*

With help from Janice and his friends, Jeff was feeling like life was worth living again. He now had a purpose. When he lost the person who made his life full, he felt he lost his heart. Through so many acts of kindness, he gained a new heart only to find out how much he loved sharing it with others.

THE END

www.ingramcontent.com/pod-product-compliance
Lightning Source LLC
Chambersburg PA
CBHW050138110726

47898CB00008B/2573